A Novel

A WORLD AWAY

MISHA CHHADA

To my family and friends.

You have all become my angels, now and forever.

ANGELEE

Winter was when my heart turned to ice and shattered into a million little pieces. It wasn't winter, yet my heart was still shattered.

All three of us sat around a wooden table—my mother, my father, and me. I stared at the birthday cake placed directly in front of me, disappointingly plain and dull. I remembered my birthdays from all the years before, colorful, joyful, elated. The cakes had been mint green or light blue, with delicate pink fondant flowers and even accents of gold leaf. My mother and father were still youthful and jovial then. I glanced at them now and studied the creases on my mother's forehead and my dad's salt-and-pepper hair.

My mother and father were considered wealthy, and they were. I had always disregarded their efforts, mostly because of how they chose to use their wealth and time. In numerous ways, they were misguided, and that showed in their actions. It wasn't that they looked down upon the less fortunate; it was that they were overly dedicated to their work, to the point of obsession. They had no time left to give—and yet somehow, they still had time to want more and more.

I sighed. I had once looked up to them, aspiring to be what they were. Yet as I had grown older, I realized they were nothing more than selfish and greedy. It was true that they worked hard for what they had, but they had little respect for the poor. They depended on a lifestyle of opulence for their pleasure. I hoped I wasn't a reflection of them. I hoped that one day, I would use my power for good.

I continued to stare at the tiny flame as the wick stopped sputtering and burned with a neon-yellow hue. I sucked in some air and exhaled. The flame lingered for a moment before turning a dark blue, then it became paler and paler, until finally it vanished.

I knew I should make a wish—and I truly wanted to—but I knew that it wouldn't change a thing. Life would go on, and yet remain the same. No one smiled or clapped or whistled or cheered—not like on my fifteenth birthday, my fourteenth birthday, or all the years before. I didn't blame my parents; there was no reason for them to be joyful. Turning sixteen should have been an achievement for me. It should have been memorable. But where we lived, it was a punishment, the end of something good.

We resided in the toe of Italy's boot in a charming region called Calabria. Calabria was split up into five equal provinces. Vibo Valentia and Catanzaro were used for industrial purposes. Crotone was where the Devils lived, and Cosenza was where the Angels lived. And the most popular province, Reggio di Calabria, had once been a popular tourist destination, but now it was home to the deserted village and beach of Scilla. It used to be a beautiful sun-drenched region of mountains and old-fashioned villages. Its picturesque coastline had once been home to many popular beaches, including Pizzo. But the sand soon became rough, the villages began to crumble, and it wasn't even worthy of a family photo anymore.

A sixteenth birthday in Calabria wasn't a celebration at all—at least, that's what my friends said. My mother tried to make it a moment to remember, but no matter how hard she tried, it would never be special. She unceremoniously handed me a knife, and I cut three equal slices of cake. None of us even bothered to eat it.

My mother noticed the awkward silence filling the room and nodded her head slightly, motioning for me to head upstairs. There was no use in me being downstairs anyway. My mother followed and stood at the foot of the stairs, observing me, perhaps. She took a deep breath, then spoke in a gentle whisper. Her voice was like a lullaby.

"Angelee. I know it's hard. I've been through it as well. But you can't blame our dictator for turning this region into what it has become. Calabria was once beautiful. You remember the story I used to tell you when you were younger?"

I was grateful that she didn't wait for a response. I didn't feel like talking, my throat dry and parched.

My mom continued, "Your great-great-great-grandma didn't have cruel parents. They just wanted the best for her. So, they arranged her marriage in Calabria, knowing that handing her off to a man was the best thing to do. She had no choice; most women didn't back then. And so, she uprooted her entire life from the small village where she lived and brought it here. From nothing, she created everything. Angelee, you remind me of her. I didn't know her personally, but from the stories I've heard, it seems as if her soul has merged with yours."

"I know, I know." I tried to block her words out, but it wasn't working.

I guess it was apparent that I needed my space, and Mother didn't say much more before leaving my bedroom.

SIERRA

I looked out the long white window in my bedroom wall, staring at the sky. The clouds promised heavy rain. I hugged my knees to my chest and rocked back and forth, trying to soothe myself and conceal my tears. It would be my sixteenth birthday tomorrow. Just another year of living without my mother; just another year in this dystopian world. For the next few moments, I sat there just staring at the horizon as the dark faded and light took over. I had once wanted to be sixteen. In fact, there was a time when that was all that I could think about. But now the thought of turning sixteen was terrifying.

A voice, gruff and scratchy, interrupted me from my somber thoughts. "Dinnertime," my father called.

I walked into the kitchen without saying a word. It was a short distance, as our apartment was small and cramped. We barely had any money, but somehow we managed to stay alive. Every day was a struggle, and every night before I fell asleep, I prayed to God that my father and I would have the strength to make it through to the next morning.

Cardboard boxes were strewn about, and I took a seat on one of them. The rough surface scratched against my tattered clothing. My father handed me a plastic bowl containing some raw beans, a piece of cold bread, and a few grains of rice. To the Angels, this meal would be considered intolerable, something fit for an

"

animal. But to the Devils, it was more food than anyone had seen in a long time.

And for me, this was what hurt so severely: I was poor, and they were rich. I had nothing, and they had everything. The Angels had everything they could wish for. They had a lavish amount of food, and they were affluent. I closed my eyes and tried to imagine what a meal would look like for them, but I would never know. I would never get the chance to experience such gourmet meals. Instead, I would spend my life outside, collecting water from small creeks, fishing for berries on waning bushes, stealing rags that could serve as clothes from nearby dumps, and glancing through large bay windows, trying to answer the only questions on my mind: What if I were an Angel? What if I were wealthy enough to afford proper clothes? What if I had the money to buy food from a store and didn't have to desperately seek it out every day?

My father couldn't fend for us himself; he was too weak. He would never survive alone in the hunting world. Hunting was where the money came from for most families. The meat could be sold in numerous places, and the Angels loved their meat. Hunting for meat was a reliable business and offered a fair amount of money in return.

Back in the day, women had been considered helpless. Now, the roles were reversed, and the women were expected to hunt for food. Groups of women were assigned specific days to hunt in the woods. Without a strict schedule, the woods would become overpopulated, too much fresh meat that would eventually spoil. The woods had once been a national park called Aspromonte, or so they said, home to wild boar and deer, similar to today. You could choose whether you wanted to sign up to go hunting, and the Angels rarely did. But the Devils always chose to hunt. The woods were only a fifteen-minute walk from our house, and so my father agreed for me to sign up. But in reality, we had no choice; it was either that or starvation.

Mondays were my assigned day to hunt. Only a few other girls shared this day with me. We would all rise before the sun did. Since it was still dark, we held onto each other for guidance. If only one of us was successful in the hunt, we would end up sharing the profits at the end of the day. We were always looking out for each other. In fact, all the Devils did. We were a close-knit community, and the Angels would never know what that was like.

The population of Calabria was fairly small; roughly two thousand people lived here. In the early-to-mid-2000s, there had been close to two hundred thousand citizens. But the population since then had declined at a rapid pace, leaving the rest of us behind in despair.

The girls I hunted with were all around my age. We kept to ourselves most of the time, and we preferred it that way. But we still stayed within close proximity of each other, in case anything went wrong. Perhaps a wild boar might become savage, or a bear might stumble upon us. We used the leftover money we received from selling the game to buy food from local vendors. Some days, we also crafted weapons, using wood harvested from the forest. Weapons were banned in Calabria, so we had to make do with what little resources we had.

In the end, hunting was the only thing that helped pay the bills. My late mother was actually the one who had taught me to hunt, and I remembered spending endless mornings with her, sitting on the pine-needle-covered forest floor. Once in a while, when Father was busy at work, we would bring an old red-and-white checkered blanket into the woods, finding a sunny patch of grass to sit on by the river's edge, gazing at the running water. Occasionally, we would consume the edible berries that we plucked off half-dead bushes. Those were my favorite days, when we would just lie in the sun and listen to the beautiful hum of the wood thrushes. Their sounds filled my mother and me with so much joy.

Sometimes when I was alone in the woods, I tried to see her—my mother. I felt her in the rustling of the wind and the rushing of water in the seemingly endless creek. I heard her in the beautiful song of the wood thrush, and I knew it was her who was singing. It was her whom I sensed every time I entered the woods. It was her who guided me when I felt overwhelmed in trying to help my father. And sometimes I whispered to her in the woods, hoping the wind would carry my message: "I love you."

ANGELEE

My mother said slowly, "I will always love you. Even if you're not mine. Even if you're someone else's daughter. Even if you belong to another mother."

I thought the comparison between my mother and me didn't matter. My eyes were the color of the ocean, and hers the color of sand. My hair was dark, and her hair was copper. Those differences didn't define us as human beings. I hoped she knew that I loved her. I hoped she knew that I would never trade her for someone else. I hoped she saw the same beauty in me that I saw in her. She had made countless mistakes, but those were in the past. I still loved her, no matter what.

I cried myself to sleep. I didn't know why, but I did. Crying wasn't weakness; it was strength, I reminded myself. I cried until I had no tears left.

SIERRA

It was morning. I had slept for seven hours. The loud croaking of the rooster had woken me up, as it did every day. I needed a few more hours of darkness, not to sleep, but to think. I needed some way to organize my disarray of thoughts. But already, I could see the chaos that covered my room—the piles of dirty clothes, the rotted desk in the corner, the flickering lamp.

I yanked back the tattered cloths that served as curtains, and light showered into every corner of my room. I stared out the window, just as I did every morning and every night. I sat there as brilliant colors painted the sky. I was not as lucky as the Angels, but at least I had the sky above me. I had my own bedroom and clothes. I had some food to keep my dad and me from dying of starvation. It wasn't the best life, but I was fine with it, and if I'd had the chance to switch lives with an Angel, I would have refused.

That said, my life was still considered harder than many others. We Devils had to work twice as hard as any Angel just to stay alive. Growing up, I had learned everything I needed from my mother: to hunt for animals in the nearby forest, to find fresh water, to fish, and to trade produce.

As a Devil, I'd had to overcome one of the saddest things anyone could ever go through: the death of a loved one. I was only eight when my mother died of a very rare sickness. There was a cure for it, of course, but the dictator didn't allow the medication to get delivered to Calabria. I blamed the dictator for my mother's death, and I knew my father did too.

I took a deep breath to gather myself and walked into the kitchen, where I saw a single slice of birthday cake and a clean white envelope. I took a seat on a hard plastic chair and opened the letter.

Happy birthday, honey! Sorry I couldn't be there to celebrate. I'll be home soon though—save a piece of cake for me!

I smiled and stared at the slice of chocolate cake with tiny coconut flakes on top. I would have preferred to celebrate with my father, but I knew he had to work to provide for us. Men did all of the work in Calabria, but still, Devil woman had to hunt in order to survive. I grabbed a plastic fork from the utensil container, which had somehow miraculously filled up overnight. I took a tiny bite of the decadent cake. I had to enjoy every second of this luxury, because the next time I would be getting it was in a year. Happiness was a luxury, luxury was money, and money was something we didn't have. I stared down at the cake, half expecting another fork to appear for my father.

The house was silent, the sun was blazing through the window, and the chair I was sitting on grew hot and stung my legs. It was summer, and flowers that were once blooming had burned to a crisp in the scorching heat. In Italy, you would have thought it would be warm all year round, but not in the 2300s. Climate change had made the summers extremely hot and the winters extremely cold.

I would not have to go to school, now or in the fall. My father had to work double shifts to afford me just a year at my local high school, and even then, it wouldn't be enough to pay for my senior year of high school or starting college. So, instead, I would stay home. Except for tomorrow.

Every year, once a child in Calabria turned sixteen, a dreadful tragedy arose. The day after their sixteenth birthday was when they took a visit to the municipal building, where they would be tested with a series of complicated exams and questions to determine who their soulmate would be. A soulmate couple could be a boy and a girl, two girls, or two boys. A soulmate wasn't associated with love; it was just someone who you were destined to be with. A person forced to you by fate, A soulmate could also be a friend, someone who would have your back for the long run. Angels didn't have to pay for their soulmate results; however, Devils had to pay nearly a fortune for theirs.

In a soulmate duo, if a girl and boy were paired together, the boy would end up as a slave or something of a peasant or servant, working countless hours in the field or in the kitchen. In a soulmate duo of two boys, both would end up contributing work, but if there was a soulmate pairing of two girls, neither of them would do any work whatsoever. The concept for the system borrowed from medieval Europe. Men were forced to work in the fields of a manor, run by a lord. They would maintain the agriculture, but receive little to no pay. Many people worked on the manor, including beekeepers to create honey and wax, blacksmiths to fabricate weapons, and serfs, who were tied to working the land, meaning they could never leave. Finally, there were the peasants, who were much like the serfs, except they could leave the manor whenever they pleased.

The soulmate system had been designed by our ruthless dictator, Fleur Toussaint. In the few years of school I had attended, we were forced to learn about Fleur, under orders given by none other than the dictator herself. Fleur had grown up in a tiny commune in France called Blesle. It was then home to only 650 residents, and the village itself was almost a complete secret, all stone cottages and sunlit alleyways and beautiful purple flowers. Growing up, Fleur had watched as women got treated much worse than men.

She saw women cleaning and cooking and performing other household tasks, while the men headed out to their jobs and spent time with their friends. Our history teacher had explained to us that there were about 350 women in the village at the time, and only four of them had a job outside the home.

When Fleur was sixteen, she had run away from home to Calabria and completed her education here. She became very powerful and worked hard for her so-called success, and in 2322, she became dictator of Calabria. Then she had created the system of soulmates, ultimately because she wanted men to suffer just as much as women once had.

I sat in a neon-green plastic chair and basked in the sun. The delicacy of the golden rays entered my coal-colored eyes and turned them hazel. I indulged in the final bite of my cake, relishing the flavor, making sure to save a rather large portion of the slice for my father.

I closed my eyes and could see phosphenes of orange through my eyelids. Dreaming was my favorite part of any day. I would often sit here in this chair when my father was at work and close my eyes; I had nothing else to do. Dreams were a different world, a new reality. Dreams were a way to escape your troubles and complications. Above all, they weren't real life. You could create friends and become a different version of yourself. Your brain could process anything, and you could be happier, and so could the people around you. This morning, my dream was about the day I had been born, exactly sixteen years ago. My mother was still alive. And my father was happy. That was long ago, that was far away now.

My father came home late last night. It was 9:00 p.m., much later than either of us expected, as he usually arrived home at 7:00 p.m. I was still awake and lying on my bed. My father knocked on my door. I didn't say anything, so he let himself in. He sat on the edge of my bed and squeezed me. "Happy birthday!" he said enthusiastically. When I didn't say anything, he frowned. "Come on, don't do that. I had to work. I have to provide for us. It's hard to be a single father."

I nodded, and this time I squeezed him back. "I know. Thank you for everything—especially the slice of cake. You knew it was my favorite."

"How could I forget? I remember when you were a little girl, and we would go on walks past the bakery. You would press your little face against the glass and try to get a whiff of the delicious aroma. You would occasionally ask me if I could buy a slice for you, but I would always say no." My father cast his eyes downward, as if ashamed.

"Dad, it's okay. You're trying. You're doing your best."

"Well, it's not enough." An edge of frustration crept into his voice. "I wish I could do more—I really do. I couldn't even afford a birthday card from the dollar store."

"It's fine. I wouldn't want anyone else in the world to replace you. It was hard when Mother died, and after that when we were left with nothing. But you were so brave, and you always put me before yourself. That takes a lot of strength."

He smiled softly. "Thanks, Si Si. Now get some rest."

I smiled back, but it faded only a moment after he closed the door.

ANGELEE

White-washed walls. White-tiled floors. An elegant room. Velvet chairs. There were rarely any other people at this time; few residents of Calabria celebrated their birthday in August. The vibration of the air conditioner relaxed me, and I was thankful for the sound rather than silence.

In the letter I had received from the municipal building days before, they had told me to wait in line at booth number four. The letter was formatted on plain white stationery, the words printed in a neat font. The letter had also explained that at exactly half past three, I would meet my assistant, who would be questioning me for the numerous exams.

It was five minutes until three. I held my breath; there was no use in breathing anymore. People said that the Angels got better soulmates than the Devils, so perhaps it wouldn't be too bad. The men would be required to attend to the day's household work, while we women would get real jobs and be given the role of head of the household. So, why did people say it was so bad? I lowered my head. It was going to be torture.

I couldn't manage to comfort myself; I was quite the pessimist. I had always been a negative thinker, but these days I felt less and less guilty for it, because now I had a reason, an explanation. Wasn't that what we all wanted: an answer to our questions? But my father hated my attitude. He told me I had once been so sweet that all the honeybees thought I was a flower, but that I had changed because of my grandmother's death.

I remembered the day when I had gone to visit her with my parents. I hadn't seen her in a long time, due to her sickness. At the hospital, nurses in navy-blue scrubs were pacing around my grandmother. There were doctors in white coats with long stethoscopes hanging around their necks. Charts and patient records dotted the room. There were whispers and tears and shouts of anger boiling over. I stood outside the doorway, watching it all through the small window, up on my toes to get a good view. It had hurt my soul, my heart, and my mind. It burned down my whole world. Yet I had to watch; I had to see my grandmother one last time.

Slowly, I had opened the door, even though I clearly wasn't supposed to. My mother was crouched by my grandmother, gentle tears rolling down her cheeks. I knelt beside my mother, and she completely ignored the fact that I shouldn't have been there; like me, she knew I had to see my grandmother one last time. My mother stood up and slowly walked away. I didn't blame her. It was hard to lose someone you loved, especially when they had been there for you your whole life. I stared at my grandmother and cried. I was only thirteen then, but I would have wept just as hard right now if I had to go through that experience again. It felt like a hurricane.

I snapped back to reality in the municipal building, and my tangled thoughts finally became one. There was now only one person ahead of me in line. The woman stood perfectly still, taking light and breezy breaths. Her blonde hair almost brushed her shoulders, and her eyes were almond-shaped, the inner corners turned slightly downwards. She seemed anxious; I could tell from her uncomfortable stance.

Suddenly, a man wearing a solid white uniform called her to one of the booths. She nervously walked over to the compartment, a large rectangular structure with plexiglass covering all but one wall. She spoke to the man for quite a while. I tried to listen in, but all I could hear were tiny snippets of the conversation. The woman was pleading with the man for a lower tax bill. She took out all the money she had in her wallet, and the man counted it with a sneer on his face and frowned.

"Ma'am, I'm going to need more. You have until tomorrow to get me the payment. Otherwise, the dictator will determine your punishment."

The woman nodded and hastily ran from the booth, all the while sobbing into her soot-covered hands.

The man shuffled some papers and prepared his office for the next person in line: me. He called me up, and for a moment, I didn't even realize it; I was caught up in my own little world. Then he called me again. I walked over to the box-shaped booth, even more slowly than the lady before me. I took a deep breath.

SIERRA

I sat in my room, dreading what tomorrow would turn out to be like. Dull and quiet—but wasn't that what I wanted? Hadn't I dreamed of this: traveling to the municipal building, answering questions, being a part of something greater than myself? When I was younger, I had eagerly awaited the day I would turn sixteen. I had longed to receive my very own soulmate and have the freedom to do whatever I desired. On my sixth birthday, I had blown out six candles, and my wish was to be sixteen. I had made the wrong wish. But when I turned fifteen, the municipal building had sent me a starched letter, which explained the selection process and offered examples of the many questions the assistants would ask. The letter had also discussed Fleur's past and her perspective on life.

Although my father and I lived in a small apartment, we had everything we needed, including our own bedrooms. And even though I had spent many winters foraging for food in the brisk temperatures, I was still very lucky to have a functioning kitchen and the ability to find winter berries anywhere. In a way, I was lucky, and yet misfortune still haunted me. Our cabinets should have been filled with food, but instead, they were now filled with nothing but crumbs and a few leftovers. The water that we drank was contaminated with lead, so we had to use a special device to filter it. The heat in our house was minimal, causing an unbearable condition in the cold winters.

In our town, we had no good form of leadership, only Dictator Fleur, and she didn't really count. On the one hand, if you compared our life to the other Devils, we would be considered rich. However, if we were compared to the Angels, we were considered poor and filthy. I recalled a time when I had asked my father the difference between the Angels and Devils, and he hesitated for a long time. He had an understanding of the world that nobody else seemed to have, yet he still couldn't answer the question. It seemed as if there was no answer.

In later years, he had told me that Fleur wanted men to get a fresh perspective on what gender inequality was like, how rough the experience was, and what it was like to go through it. Father told me that Fleur had made men suffer because of this, to the point where many Devils and even some Angels were dying.

Father had talked to me about so much, and it was often difficult for me to understand him. I had sat on his lap and wrapped my arms around his neck as he hugged me, and I watched as tears ran down his face. I remembered clutching my lavender-scented teddy bear tightly to my chest, asking, "Daddy, why are you crying?" He had looked into my eyes and grabbed a spare tissue from his torn jacket pocket, sniffling into its rough texture. He then told me that everything would be okay, and that everyone cried sometimes. I was six then, and too young to know what sorrow truly felt like. I had tried to soothe my father, although I had no understanding of the reason behind his tears. My father thought I had paid little to no attention to the death of my mother when I was younger. Little did he know that it was all I could think about.

When I was twelve, a question had occurred to me that would haunt me in later years: was it my fault that my mother had died? Did she leave the world because I entered it? I remembered gathering the courage to ask my father this. He had propped me up in his lap, just as he did when I was six, and he told me something I would never forget: It wasn't my fault. I was a gift. I was another version of my mother. And yet, I was also Sierra. This was no Devil's act; in fact, he told me there was no such thing as a Devil. Everyone had a bit of good in their souls; they just had different ways of covering it up. I looked straight at him in that moment and smiled. It felt good, mostly because I hadn't been happy in a long, long time.

ANGELEE

The man standing at the booth in a plain white uniform had a golden badge placed right on top of his heart that said, MARESCIALLO. I knew Italian, yet I never spoke it in Calabria. Most of the citizens who lived here spoke English, as they came from faraway places. My biological parents had taught me some of the language before I was put up for adoption. I knew that the word on the man's badge meant "marshall." Even the men who were forced into labor were loyal to our dictator—or maybe they just had no other option. Perhaps they were fearful of punishment; execution wasn't rare.

The man had a thick Italian accent. I was finding it rather difficult to understand anything beyond his tone. I took a deep breath. I had received a letter last year about some of the test questions they would be asking, but I wasn't at all prepared. Luckily, the first few questions were quite easy. The marshall needed some form of identification, but I didn't have a driver's license because in Calabria, cars were rather rare, and you had to be eighteen to drive anyway. So, I showed the man my passport instead. There were no stamps on it, because no one in Calabria could ever leave the region; it was strictly forbidden.

Maresciallo Dimitri examined my passport very scrupulously. He studied each and every word and number, and after what seemed like forever, he nodded, as if to tell me I had passed in some way.

After the identification was complete, the man directed me to a room in the very back of the building. I turned the doorknob and entered the room. The lighting was harsh, with many pops of color smeared on the walls. There was a single bed in the corner of the room with no mattress, just a bare black frame. Other than that, the room was empty, and the floor was bare concrete. I didn't know exactly what or whom I was waiting for, but I didn't want to sit on the cold metal bed, so I just stood there expectantly.

I was left alone with my thoughts, and it felt like hours must have ticked by. I didn't want to think about time, when I knew there would be so much of it in my future—so much time that would be wasted. Life would go on, cold and relentless. Time would creep past me slower and slower, and then I would eventually die. What would happen after that? What would happen before that? Only time would tell—and that was the problem. I wanted less and less of it. There was no point in having more time in this sorrowful life of mine.

I remembered sitting in English class in sixth grade. My teacher would always teach us a word of the day. I had walked into her room one chilly December morning as she was writing a word I had never seen before on the whiteboard. A few moments later, when everybody was seated at their desks, she read out the word to us. "Sonder. Does anyone know what that means?" No one responded. So, our teacher went on, "*Sonder* is a fascinating word. Surprisingly, it's a noun. And you may have never heard of it, because it isn't in the actual dictionary." My fellow students weren't listening. She continued nevertheless, "Sonder is the realization that each person you meet has their own life as vivid and complex as yours. The reason I chose this word was not only to help with your vocabulary, but to help you realize that everyone around you has been through sadness and pain. It's okay to feel bad at times, especially living under the rule of our dictator. I know things have been hard for all of you, but I want you to know that we're all here for you." She motioned around the room and sighed, "We always will be."

My teacher had essentially risked her job by saying this, just to make us feel welcome in this ugly world.

Back in the real world, footsteps echoed down the hall, and a plump woman entered the room. She had waist-length hair and wore thick-rimmed glasses that nearly hid her long, spidery eyelashes, along with an oversized sweatshirt and black leggings. To my surprise, she had an American country accent that could only be heard when she said certain words.

"Hi, my name is Darlene. Yours is Angelee? Anyway, I understand you're here for the tests?" It seemed to be a rhetorical question, because she continued without waiting for an answer. "Good, because you're going to be taking several of them, hon. They should be pretty easy, and if you ask me, they're stupid questions. I don't know how Fleur came up with this nonsense."

She talked about the dictator like they were old friends, referring to her by her first name and occasionally giving her odd nicknames.

"Hon, you listening?" I nodded, and she continued with satisfaction, "Okay. I'm going to read a question out loud. Just try and answer with only a couple of words. We want this to be quick and easy, alright? So, first question: what are the best qualities in a person?"

I raised an eyebrow. "Why exactly does the dictator want to know this?"

"I have no say in the questions; these were orders given to me directly by her. I'm guessing she wants to help you find your perfect soulmate that possesses all the attributes you describe.

Let's continue, alright? Next question: what is one thing you could never go without? Besides necessities."

"Will Fleur be able to tell if I'm lying?" I asked cautiously.

"Oh, Fleur can always tell when someone is being dishonest."

"Fine. I guess it's my parents."

"Okay, good! Now we're getting somewhere. Next up…" Darlene peered more closely through her partially cracked glasses at the paper she was holding. "What motivates you to work hard, and why?"

"I think I'm self-motivated. I draw on my own problems to push me further."

"Okay, two more. What is your biggest fear?"

"I guess losing somebody. Also, I was once afraid of turning sixteen," I said in a small voice.

Darlene raised her glasses and looked at me sympathetically. Then her eyes turned cold and dark and empty. She cleared her throat. "Well then, we'd better get going."

"I thought you said we had one more question left."

"Not anymore you don't. Please follow me to the next room."

I followed her down a wide hallway, leading to a room that was plain and white. There was a single chair, and a machine that looked unworldly—a machine so high-tech that I would never have expected to see it in the little region of Calabria. Other than that, the room was bare.

"I want you to have a seat right here." Darlene motioned to the tan reclining chair, sort of like what you'd see in a dentist's office.

Hesitating, I took a seat. It felt soft and comfortable—probably just another of the dictator's tricks to ease us into her sinister plan.

Darlene frowned. "I haven't worked this machine yet. Usually I use the machine in the other room. Where are the instructions?"

I tried to see past Darlene's pudgy body. She was blocking the view, but I hadn't noticed a pamphlet of instructions anywhere. Then she moved aside and gave me a better look at the machine. It was a dull gray, and it looked as if it had never been used. Darlene explained, "I assume this machine has the same purpose as the one I normally use, even if it looks a little different. It will scan your eyes for forensic purposes."

I hadn't committed a crime, of course; the data from the scan would be used to find a match for me. The machine was basically a cube with little tubes sprouting out of it, like the branches of a tree, except less aesthetically pleasing. Each tube held a mysterious elixir in different shades of blue. Darlene explained about the tubes, sharing that they were a source of electricity for the machine. There were also several lenses on the front. The process of the machine scanning my eyes was complex, yet Darlene assured me it would take no time at all. It seemed as if she was finally figuring out how to operate the machine, as it was quite similar to the old one.

First, I had to prepare my eyes for the scan. Darlene dripped several drops of a medical solution into my eyes, so the scan could view the internal structures. Next, she set up the machine by typing various codes and phrases into the database. Finally, she told me, the machine would use several camera lenses to scan my eyes, and then it would take a while to collect the information and process it. But overall, the actual test would be over quite quickly.

Darlene began the first procedure. She opened her leather purse and pulled out a small bottle: the formula that would help the machine see the interior of my eyes. She dropped the formula into my eyes and it felt frigid, yet refreshing. It was satisfying to feel the cold against my sun-kissed skin.

Darlene smiled. "Feels good, doesn't it?" She placed the formula back in her purse and turned to the complex machine. There were many buttons on the top, but no labels indicating what each was designed to do. Darlene investigated the room again for a booklet or a brochure—anything at all that might contain instructions. Maybe I was wrong; maybe she didn't know what she was doing. I watched as she took a deep breath and tried to collect herself. Then out of nowhere, she screamed loudly in a very high pitch. The scream was short, but it could certainly be heard throughout the building, and for a moment, I felt as if I were watching an opera, like the fancy Italian ones I used to go to with my mother.

In moments, a man entered the room. He was holding a clipboard with a single piece of paper, filled with scribbled notes in the margins. He put on some glasses and peered disapprovingly at Darlene. She rolled her eyes and smacked her lips together, chewing some sort of fruit-flavored gum. "Hon, do you need something?"

The man responded in a stern voice, "I was just about to ask you the same thing. I heard your scream. What's going on?"

"Then it worked! I needed to get your attention." She laughed playfully.

"Well, that's one way to do it…" he grumbled. "Anything to do with the technology? I've been hired as the building's IT guy by the dictator herself."

"Well, isn't that nice?" Darlene said sarcastically. "Yes, I need help logging into this machine. It's impossible."

"Okay, let me see what I can do. But just a heads up: it's gonna take at least half an hour, so I suggest you find something to do in the meantime."

"Half an hour is quite a while," she sighed. "What is there to do? Fleur strictly forbids any breaks while we're supposed to be working. It's not like there's an arcade in the building. And we're already behind schedule; people are probably waiting!"

"Actually, the lines outside are pretty short today."

"Oh, that's definitely a surprise! I guess August is the least busy time of the year for us." Darlene shook her head, as if she had finally remembered something of value. "We could probably sneak out, if you cover for us. But where would we go?"

"Right. Why don't you two just go to the coffee shop down the road?"

"But there are no coffee shops. At least, not since Fleur's been in charge."

"Do you not know what's happening around Calabria?" he sputtered. "Fleur has been opening a whole bunch of clothing shops, fancy cafés, grocery stores, public libraries, and even theaters. She wants to gain more popularity, and she's reopened the stores to gain more followers, more power. But the stores are only open to women. She wants the women to respect her, just as she respects them."

"That is the stupidest thing I've ever heard," Darlene grumbled. "Why does she want to gain popularity? She's supposed to be our dictator, not a teenage girl looking for attention. She's unpredictable, truly. I don't even know why she makes women go through the torture of pairing up with soulmates, if she's supposedly also fighting for them?"

"She knows how hard women can work," he said. "She knows their strength, and she knows they'll be able to withstand the torture of soulmate pairings. Anyway, I gotta get to fixing this machine. And if anyone asks where you are, I'll say you're in the bathroom."

"Thank you for everything," she said, clearly relieved. "I didn't catch your name. Mine's Darlene."

"Yep, I could tell; you're the loud one. My name's Lamonte."

"Well, thank you, Lamonte."

Darlene retrieved her light fleece from a small cupboard in the corner of the room. She slipped it on along with a winter hat. I stifled a laugh at this; it was the middle of summer. She then beckoned me to follow her out into the network of hallways, each one white and bare, until we reached a large brass door with a golden knocker. There was a heavy-looking silver keypad on the door that contained all the numbers from zero to one hundred. Darlene paused and retrieved a small piece of paper that was barely big enough to contain the code. It must have been five minutes before she finished, and then it took another five minutes, because she somehow managed to delete a string of numbers she had previously entered. She sighed in frustration and cursed under her breath.

Finally, the door opened, and I could feel the fresh air upon my face. At least this was something the dictator could never take away. The air smelled salty like the bitter ocean breeze, not too sweet, but peachy and earthy, like after a fire. It was raining outside. The scent of the rainwater contributed to the smell of the earth.

As Darlene and I walked out into the pouring rain, few cars drove past us. Many roads were reserved for the purposes of the dictator, so many streets that had once been home to cozy and sweet little stores were now closed. There was no point in driving. In fact, there wasn't much point in doing anything. The rain got heavier, and now my whole outfit was soaked to the point where I felt like I had just drowned in the Mediterranean Sea.

There was no conversation between Darlene and me. Instead, we focused our attention on the shops that had just opened. Lamonte had explained that this street and two others were the only ones in Calabria that were home to accessible stores. Lavish restaurants now dotted Giulio Camuzzoni Street. There were also petite boutiques and cafés that smelled of eclairs, tiramisu, and those little fried dough balls filled with custard or raspberry compote and sprinkled with powdered sugar.

My feet were now aching. My body wasn't really accustomed to exercise because I was forced to spend my free time in my house. Thankfully, we soon stopped at a small coffee shop on the corner. The exterior of the building was painted white, contrasting with the black frames of the freshly cleaned windows. Small marmalade-colored bouquets were arranged in a gorgeous array by the white front door, and small wooden barstools were situated by the window to offer outdoor seating.

Darlene opened the door and held it open as I made my way inside the cozy café. The interior was much like the outside: clean and minimalist. There was a seating area with comfy lounge chairs and sectionals, and the accent wall had a wooden herringbone design. The other end of the room was reserved for employees. There was a large glass shelf holding an array of treats and delights, including rainbow cookies and an assortment of bananas and mangos. Behind the counter was a space solely dedicated to the art of coffee, with porcelain cups, packets of Splenda, and small biscotti placed neatly in white jars.

Darlene studied the menu and then surveyed the scones. In the end, she chose a blueberry-lemon scone. I'd had enough for the day, and my appetite was slowly fading away, so I told the employee I didn't want anything. But Darlene insisted she would buy me something, and that she wouldn't let me go back to the municipal building until my stomach was full. I couldn't refuse, so I gave in and ordered an herbal tea with warm, crusty bread and a side of melted butter.

Darlene was satisfied as she watched me eat small nibbles of my food and soon reopened the conversation. "Well, we're here, so we might as well have you answer one more question while we wait on Lamonte. Let's see…" She repositioned her askew glasses back over her chartreuse eyes and skimmed the small piece of paper covered with many questions. "Okay, the question is, if you had a chance to go back in time, what would you do?"

SIERRA

Ruby-red blood. My mother was lying in a hospital bed, monitors beeping, doctors and nurses rushing in and out. My dad was crying. I watched this through the small window in the door. More doctors now. I still watched. My mother was trying to camouflage her pain. There was anxiety, stress.

I entered the room. My mom smiled wearily. My dad was sobbing, yelling, screaming. My mother held me, clutching me ever so tightly. Then my dad gently plucked me out of my mother's arms and kissed me on my head. He kissed my mother too.

When we were leaving the hospital, I couldn't help thinking that my mother was dead, and I was alive. My father told me that I was a gift, another version of my mother, but I believed that less and less every day. I was a Devil, born and raised. I would never be an Angel. My mother was an angel though—not because of her wealth, but because of her attributes, everything that defined her. She was *my* angel, even though I had known her for less than a decade of my life.

When you lose someone, the pain hurts less and heals faster when you have another person by your side. But in this case, the agony tore me apart, even though my father was going through it as well. We rarely talked about the death of my mother; my father avoided the subject at all costs. There were a few times when I asked about her, but he didn't hear, or at least pretended not to.

I would have liked to know her better, or at least know more about her. I had only ever managed to gather a few facts about her from my father.

ANGELEE

Darlene waited for me to answer the question. I knew that she was hoping for a reasonable answer, but I couldn't give it to her. I needed more time.

Darlene was beginning to get impatient. She returned to the counter and asked for an espresso; perhaps she needed to stay awake. Once she sat back down, I took a deep breath and said, "I would just stay in this moment. There's nothing I would ever do differently."

Darlene smiled. "That's one of the most pleasant responses I've heard in a long time. I was getting impatient, but you should never rush good things." She winked. "Anyway, let's go. I think Lamonte should be done by now. That machine is one ding-dang piece of work." She gathered up her purse and thick cashmere sweater. "Ready?"

We walked along the damp cobblestone road back to the municipal building. The dim glow of the streetlamps stained the streets with an eerie atmosphere. It had stopped raining now, but the clouds were still dark gray, crowding the once-vivid blue sky.

Darlene offered me a bright yellow umbrella, but I declined. Throughout my life, I had loved the rain. We walked on and on, passing by another café and a seamstress shop. But Darlene's eyes widened when she stumbled across a bead shop. She smiled and started laughing out of nowhere, sweet and melodic. It was the sound of happiness and childhood. "We still have time, right? My mother used to own a bead shop, and it looked just like this one! You don't mind if we take a look, do you?"

I nodded; it was fine by me. Even though I just wanted to get the soulmate testing over with, I didn't mind if we stopped for a bit.

The shop was quite modestly sized, and almost every nook and cranny was filled with some piece of junk. Darlene smiled and strolled around the shop, as if she were familiar with it. She examined almost everything. There were many plastic containers lined up against a colorful wall, holding hundreds of beads, some small, some big, both colorful and plain. Each container held only one type of bead, and the owner clearly planned to keep it that way. She must have gotten up early every morning to make sure each bead was in its proper place. Besides the solid-colored beads, there were hundreds of varieties: bugles, chatons, Rivoli, Delica, Rocaille, Shambala, and more. Darlene stared at the bugle beads longer than any of the others, and I could tell they were her favorite. The beads were tubular, cut to various lengths, but the width was consistent.

Darlene and I were observing some of the beads in an aisle in the back of the store when Dictator Fleur walked in.

My heart skipped a beat. My parents had taught me ever since I was a kid that if I came into contact with Dictator Fleur, I should keep to myself. Don't hide. Don't crouch. Don't talk. Don't move.

Fleur was talking worriedly with the owner of the store. I had never seen her anxious before, and I wondered if she was just like everyone else and felt the emotions that others felt daily. Sometimes I forgot that she was human too. She was wearing a pale blue shirt and pants. Her long coat was thin and made of an expensive fabric. I could tell because I was an Angel, just like she was.

The dictator sighed. "There's already been an escape," she was saying. "I'm worried that my sister's dreams are slowly slipping through my fingers."

"An escape?"

"Yes, just last night. We have cameras everywhere, but they managed to get hold of a boat and take off. It was one of the fishermen. He left, alone, at two a.m. People think I'm a villain, but I'm only doing this for Chantelle. This is what she would've wanted."

"It's not your fault, Madam."

"It is. If Chantelle were here, she would be so disappointed. This was everything for her. She wanted the world to be kinder. Why is it so cruel all of a sudden?"

"Ah, and you're asking me as if I should know," the shopkeeper said. Fleur chuckled.

"And one more thing," the dictator said. "Is my bracelet ready?"

The shopkeeper nodded and handed the dictator a bracelet with elegant lampwork beads, which had been worked directly over a fragile flame. Fleur received the bracelet graciously and smiled. For a moment, I thought I saw tears, but it might have only been a reflection.

As soon as Darlene and I left the bead shop, the rain began to come down even more heavily. We couldn't run; the cobblestones were too slippery. So, we shielded ourselves under the bright yellow umbrella. The rain dropped like heavy marbles, accelerating from the dark-gray clouds.

Getting soaked, I sprinted down a dark alley, a shortcut to the municipal building, lined with leafy trees. Once I reached our destination, I waited and waited outside of the municipal building, finally realizing that Darlene had not followed me. Where was she? I waited for what felt like hours on end, and still she didn't show up. Finally, I decided it was best to just walk into the building and wait in the eye-scanning room.

A rush of warm air tousled my hair as I entered the building. There were networks of hallways. There was no possible way I could find my way around this place without Darlene. Then I spotted a marble plaque placed above two vases of flowers, identifying the appropriate floors for various services. The municipal building not only served as the soulmate testing center, but was also where official government meetings were held. It was also one of Fleur's homes. The first floor was mainly for council meetings, but other meetings were held there as well. There was also a room for executions. The second floor was strictly for soulmate testing and administrative business. The third floor was where Fleur lived.

No one knew much about the living space that she occupied most of the time. The rumor was that there were twenty rooms —modest when compared to other leaders' accommodations— including six bedrooms, four full bathrooms, two kitchens, three living areas, and five other rooms whose uses were unknown. When I was little, I used to fall asleep imagining the luxuries held in each of the five mystery rooms. Heated indoor pools with bubbling Jacuzzi jets? Delicate pieces of China and hand-painted teacups…? But oddly enough, Fleur never bragged about her wealth. That was what surprised me the most about her. She usually kept to herself, wandering the streets, or she stayed in the municipal building. At least, that was what I had heard.

The elevator I took to the second floor was very spacious. The entire box was crystal clear, so when you looked down, you could watch as everything and everyone grew smaller and smaller. I took a deep breath and gathered my thoughts before I stepped out into the floor below Fleur's. I waited in the lobby for several minutes, gazing at the beautiful architecture. The ceiling was arched at the entrance, and there were white wooden beams all across it that hung gracefully. Delicate chains held dangling golden chandeliers.

There was no need to check in again, so I walked down one of the hallways, choosing randomly. I really wished I had Darlene here with me. *Darlene, where are you?*

I must have walked through about seven different hallways before I felt completely lost. It was as if Fleur didn't want me to take the stupid test. Why hadn't Darlene and I chosen to stay with Lamonte? Why did we have to leave?

It felt like I had been running from my problems for ages. I had to stop, I had to rest, I had to breathe. I sat down and bent my knees to my chest, cradling myself and rocking back and forth like a rocking chair. I couldn't even think straight, my thoughts tangled and twisted like my mother's jewelry. Sometimes the weight of the world was too much. But I couldn't afford to take a break; this was my day to be assigned a soulmate, and for better or for worse, I would accept it.

I stood up and pulled myself together, but didn't dare take a step forward. Maybe I was afraid, or maybe I was just not strong enough. My mind wanted me to move, but my heart wouldn't let me. Why?

I headed down the hallway, another step, and then another. I was getting close; I could feel it. I kept going until I finally reached a familiar hallway, the one I had first come through. The carpets and walls were white. Then I came across a door marked with a gold plaque: 9.

I entered the room, which was empty. I imagined Lamonte would be arriving in a few minutes. *He must have taken a bathroom break,* I told myself. But I waited a while, and no one came. I paced around the room anxiously, as I just wanted to get the testing over with.

I waited a few more moments just to make sure no one was coming before I walked over to the eye-scanning machine and decided to take a look at it. There were hundreds of buttons on the boxy piece of machinery, with no way of knowing each button's purpose. They were all different sizes, shapes, and colors, the majority of them round. There were also some levers and some purple triangular buttons. Studying the machine more closely, I realized with surprise that there were no red buttons. In my mind, red meant danger, so that must mean this piece of machinery could do no harm. I closed my eyes and moved my finger in random directions. Finally, my finger came to a halt, and I opened my eyes.

My finger was positioned above a neon-green circular button. Without even thinking, without even the tiniest bit of hesitation, I pressed the button. Nothing happened. I waited. Still nothing. Then there was a tiny whirring sound, like a record spinning on a record player. The noise got louder and louder. A small black screen on the top of the box flashed with bold blood-red letters: SIT IN THE RECLINER. I immediately obeyed, as if I were in some sort of trance. But this wasn't hypnosis; it was just my mind telling me not to listen to my heart.

The indescribable noise was getting even louder now at an accelerated rate. The world was spinning, my heart rate was increasing with every second that passed, and my mind was racing. The memories all came rushing back—except they weren't mine. I didn't recognize any of the little snippets of time that were now bottled up inside my brain.

There was a girl, in a pale white flowing nightgown. She stood next to a window, staring up at a sky full of stars, which in turn stared down upon her. She was crying, gentle tears. Yet her face remained emotionless, and no part of her moved. The moon could now be seen as the clouds drifted apart. She gave a slight smile and sat on the very edge of her bed.

Then there was screaming, and mobs of people could be seen outside the girl's window, mostly women carrying signs and shouting. The girl was smiling—not in a warm or gentle way, but eerily, mysteriously.

The fact that I could see this scared me. I didn't want to see any more; I was done. There were random strangers in my head, and I didn't know anything about them or what they had to do with me. It was as if I were a ghost, and all of my thoughts had gone, replaced with someone else's, though my body was still here. I was still Angelee, right?

I looked down. My clothes had been replaced with a white nightgown. The world stopped spinning, the noise stopped whirring, and I stopped with them. I sat there petrified in the tan recliner for several minutes. I didn't know what had happened; I was lost. I could still think the thoughts of Angelee, and I knew I was Angelee. I just felt farther than I ever had from her, from me.

I was wearing the strange girl's clothes. Shaking, I examined a strand of my hair. It was ash blonde, and thinner than my true darker hair.

I was the girl now.

I wanted to scream so badly, but I kept it within me. Even though I was someone else now, my habits were still the same; I continued to keep my anxiety bottled up and out of sight. I felt like an idiot.

I raced out of the room. I couldn't deal with this alone; I had to tell someone that I had become someone else. I was desperately in need of help—but I couldn't find anyone. I needed Darlene or Lamonte; maybe they could fix me, help me, change me back. I frantically raced from one hallway to the next. I was losing hope and very close to giving up when I heard quiet murmurs coming from a nearby hallway. I rushed in that direction, then inched my way towards where the sound was coming from.

A door was slightly ajar, and I could hear that only two people were in the room. I shifted closer, peered through the opening, and saw a woman, but could not see the other from this angle. The strangers were deep in conversation. I knew I needed help, so I took a deep breath and silently pushed the door open wider. I could now see who the woman was talking to: Dictator Fleur. My stomach dropped.

There was no way I could go into the little room and speak to Fleur in her fancy blue overcoat. She could have me executed. But at the same time, I had no choice; somehow, I was someone else. I took a deep breath and mustered some courage. I was surprised at how easy it was, but maybe it was because I was becoming that ghostly, sinister girl. Maybe that girl had courage and strength and perseverance, unlike me.

The moment I took a step inside, Fleur spun around and snapped at me, "Little girl, what are you—" She stopped mid-sentence, frozen. She stared at me, and there were delicate tears forming in her eyes. Then she shook her head, her tears gone as quickly as they had come. "What's your name, child?"

I replied rather suddenly, "I'm Fleur." Then I gasped, my eyes widening. I was Angelee … wasn't I?

Fleur rolled her eyes. "Don't joke with me, darling. If this is a prank, you should know better. I'll have you executed by daybreak if this childish behavior continues. Understood?"

I nodded, biting my lip.

"What's your real name, then?" Fleur demanded.

I wanted to say "Angelee" so badly. But I couldn't. She tapped her fingers, waiting for me to speak, her patience waning. Rage was sure to follow.

Luckily, at that moment, I noticed a small scrap of paper on the floor. I picked it up. Fleur questioned my movements, but I ignored her and instead asked her for a pen. I took it gratefully and wrote a simple sentence in a flowery cursive. I had never known how to write like this. Maybe it was because I was no longer Angelee; I was a stranger, an alien.

I wrote on the paper that my name was Angelee. Fleur shook her head, and the tears burst out again. I had heard that our dictator was strong and fearless. I had heard she had the roar of a lion. This time, her courage was expressed through her tears. Without another word, Fleur ran out of the room, sobbing.

The other woman who had been talking to Fleur strode over to me. "She's different, Fleur, isn't she? My name's Valli."

I cut her off; I didn't have time for this. "Sorry, Valli, but I need your help. I've turned into someone else! I think I know why Fleur was crying: I'm her, only when she was younger."

She frowned. "What do you mean, you're Fleur?"

"I pressed a random button on the soulmate machine, and it told me to sit in the recliner. It was as if I was under a spell. I sat in it, and this whirring noise sounded. It got louder and louder, and I drifted away faster and faster, and… This is not who I am! I have someone else's memories in my head! They're not mine—none of them!"

Valli froze, looking nauseous and dizzy. I gazed into her pupils, and they took me to another dimension. Through her eyes, the world looked as if it were spinning round and round. She looked like she had been on a long voyage at sea, and her face was almost green. I had no idea why she was getting so anxious when I was the one who was experiencing the fear and confusion. Why did Fleur and Valli seem sick, when *I* was the one under this spell? I rolled my eyes and charged out of the room.

I had to catch up with Fleur. When we were in the bead shop, I had noticed she was wearing high heels, which should make catching up with her easier. Exiting the building to the road outside, which twisted like an old strand of fishing line, I ran swiftly, hoping to find her in the pouring rain.

Up ahead, I saw a faint shadow, tall, with a soft frame. I could tell it was a woman. Her hair was long, straight, and silky, reaching halfway down to her hips. I inched closer to the shadow. There was another curve in the road ahead, so I couldn't quite make out the owner of the silhouette. But as I neared, I knew it was Fleur.

The rain was soaking the dictator and her extravagant attire. Her tears seemed to have quieted, but perhaps that was only because they were camouflaged by the harsh storm. She was positioned in an awkward way, sitting on the thoroughly soaked earth. I watched her for quite a while. Though my situation was urgent, for some reason, the Fleur in me wanted to let the dictator have her moment.

I supposed Fleur was sobbing because when she saw me—or rather, when she saw herself—it reminded her of her past. From the anecdote she had told the storekeeper of the bead shop, I could tell Fleur's younger years had not been the most pleasant. Finally, the dictator's sorrow gradually came to a stop. I walked over slowly to where she was sitting. I didn't want to rush her emotions.

"Dictator Fleur, I'm sorry," I began. "I… Well, when I first arrived to take my soulmate test, I met Darlene, and then a whole bunch of things happened. I have no idea where she is right now. I was looking for her because I wanted to get the test over with. But then I pressed a random button on the eye-scanning machine … and I turned into your younger self. I have your thoughts, your memories, your looks. I had this one memory of you in this white nightgown, and you were staring out the window. There was an angry mob of people, mostly women, and they were carrying huge signs and shouting. It was all so confusing.… Could you just help me?" I asked quietly.

Fleur's face was emotionless, a hole, just blank. "I also owe you an apology—well, to pretty much everyone. I'm sorry for everything, and for being a dictator. I honestly thought I was doing everything for the greater good, and I can't even imagine how blind I've been in the past. It's like I just woke up from a nightmare. I can see clearly now; the clouds are gone. And I'm sorry for being so emotional. It was hard to see myself from the past; I've changed so much. But that young girl staring back at me, she was bold and fearless and courageous. I'm none of those things now. My dream after my sister died was to carry on her legacy. I wanted to stop all of this inequality—but I changed for the worse. I was kind and considerate before. What's happened to me? When I saw myself through you, I remembered how my dreams first came to be. I remembered how my passions began."

After she had finished, I whispered softly, "So, you'll help me?"

The dictator chuckled softly—a sweet laugh I had never heard from her before. "Yes, of course. But I have to call a man named Aryan. He lives somewhere in between San Marino and Vatican City. He's one of the only people alive who has a cure for this. I don't even know it happened. No button on the machine has that purpose." She frowned.

But I just nodded gratefully. "I'm fine with however long it takes, as long as we get the antidote, or whatever it takes to reverse this."

With a decisive nod, Fleur took out her phone and dialed Aryan. He picked up almost immediately, and I could hear snippets of the conversation. None of what I heard meant much to me, but maybe that was for the best. Sometimes it was better to not know anything; then you wouldn't be afraid or let down. I sucked in cool wisps of air, and even though I knew I was safe in the presence of Fleur, oh, how I wished Darlene or Lamonte were by my side now.

I wondered where my parents even were. Presumably, they were busy and wouldn't have any time to spend with me, even though my birthday had just passed. I didn't blame them. They had to work, had to provide and put food on the table, so we could remain Angels. I couldn't just call them or text them, as there was no communication technology allowed in the region of Calabria, other than within the municipal building. Fleur, on the other hand, clearly played by her own rules.

I waited patiently as the dictator continued talking with Aryan. Then she hung up, biting her lip. I couldn't tell from her expression whether she was happy or scared or just nervous; our dictator was a challenging person to read. Then Fleur looked at me with her ocean-blue eyes in a sincere way and smiled slightly." Aryan will be arriving here soon. Unfortunately, the ride from Vatican City will take at least two hours."

I groaned in frustration. Two hours was a long time, especially for someone like me, who needed medical or scientific attention right away. But I was surprised by Fleur's lack of anxiety. She seemed so calm, like a sturdy boat on a placid river. She might have been desperate to fix real-world problems, but I admired how she seemed to always keep her cool in frustrating situations and find a way to circumvent those frustrations. As for me, I was everything but that, not the least bit patient. I was like a flower bud, so very eager to bloom into something beautiful. But in order to do that, I had to go through the entire process first. My mother always told me that there were no shortcuts in life, and that was torture.

I had no idea what I would do for the next couple hours. I couldn't go back home, nor did I want to; my parents would freak out. I couldn't spend the time with Darlene, because I had no idea where she was. Perhaps I could spend my spare time admiring the Calabrian landscape, something that would never get old.

Fleur strode over to me and began speaking very rapidly, as if she were in a rush. "Angelee? I have a lot of business to get through, and I need to catch up on a bunch of paperwork. Just tell me what you're doing, so I know where to find you once Aryan delivers the cure."

Fleur seemed like she was in a rush and had many things to do. I couldn't keep her waiting, so I told her I would be on Giulio Camuzzoni Street, exploring all the new little bakeries, boutiques, and shops. Fleur nodded. Then she offered me her blue coat to cover up my nightgown, which I gratefully accepted. Before I even got a chance to wave farewell, she was out of sight.

Just like Fleur had, I took off down Giulio Camuzzoni Street, past the white brick wall, past the *policia*, past the evergreens and burgundy flowers. And finally, everything came crashing down on me. With no one to save me, I sank into these dark depths, Everyone else was gone from the picture; it was just me. I couldn't hear the passing chatter of the residents of Calabria; it was just me, frozen in time. I felt like I was sinking, and I couldn't pull myself up. I had no idea which direction was which.

I wasn't a child under anyone's watchful eye now; I was alone and desperate and helpless, like I had always been. My parents were not there for me, Darlene had disappeared, Fleur had more important things to do, and I wasn't even there for myself. Visions of my life flashed before my eyes, and I realized I was holding my breath. The oxygen deprivation was taking everything away from me—my family, my thoughts, and my longing for the love no one had ever given me. Weren't people to supposed to save you if you were drowning? My head had once been on land, but now it was underwater. Why was I stuck down here when I could've been up above, swimming in a salty and summery lake? Why was I drowning when people were all around me? Why weren't they saving me?

I realized I had been so caught up with my own dense, miserable thoughts that I had paused while everyone else around me was moving, and I was still in the same spot. I had to keep going. I had been given this life for a reason, and I was strong enough to live it. I could move forward; I had always been able to. I'd just never had that faith in myself. I pushed myself forward in baby steps, as if I were just learning to walk.

I decided to go back home, just for the night. When the morning arrived, my mind would be in a much better place.

The rain stung my face. The atmosphere no longer smelled of peaches and fresh earth, but more of rotten lemons and orange zest.

If only I could escape all my problems. If only I could run away. If only I could escape Calabria. Perhaps I would go during the night, when no one was awake, and the sky full of thousands of stars would light my path to the docks that led to the Mediterranean Sea. Perhaps I would go to America. My parents probably wouldn't even realize I was missing—and when they did find out, in the end, would they even care?

I wanted to be gone. I wanted to be done with them all—my family, whose standards I could never live up to; my friends, who I never really had; my country, which had betrayed me; and myself, who was never there when I needed her most. I was sick, literally and figuratively. I was sick of always wanting to please people. But I didn't care anymore about what people thought of me. I didn't even like myself—and maybe that was why I had wanted so badly for others to like me.

I didn't care anymore about anyone or anything. It was such a peculiar sensation. I had been alone for so long, living in my mind while everyone else was living in the moment. I was frozen and lonely. But I was so used to being solitary that I realized I didn't need anyone. My parents often traveled together on lavish business trips and spent most of their spare time on work calls. In those long moments without them, I would do my own laundry and make my own food. I knew I could take care of myself.

I had never been scared of growing up, while other children had nightmares about it. But they had never lived a life alone like I had. I was never scared of living alone, because my parents were rarely available. I had practically lived alone for most of my life. If I did run away, I would simply get a job, maybe find an apartment, and take care of all my own household tasks. I realized, it wouldn't be that hard to escape the problems that kept my back bending under a colossal weight.

Once I reached home, I immediately ran to my room, careful to hide my changed appearance from my parents for fear of their reactions.

After a good night's rest, I finally returned to the bead shop the next morning, I tried to peek in through the floor-to-ceiling windows, but the glass jars of beads lining the aisles obstructed my view. I entered the store, and the door made a cheerful jingling sound, like a reindeer on Christmas Eve.

The shopkeeper smiled and greeted me pleasantly. "Hello! Welcome to String of Things. I'm Donna," she said, offering me a batch of *cuccidati*, Sicilian cookies stuffed with figs, usually served during the holiday season. With their crumbly pastry dough sprinkled with bits of sugar, these were one of my favorite Italian sweets. I gratefully accepted the gift, and the shopkeeper grinned.

"I was here before, with Darlene," I noted as I ate my cookie.

She looked puzzled. "But … I thought…"

I cut her off mid-sentence. "Something happened," I began. There was silence as I tried to talk through mouthfuls of the addictive Sicilian cookies.

Donna interrupted. "Hon, there's no need to rush or tell me what happened with your new look. I completely get it. Sometimes we just need to feel good about ourselves, right? So, what are you here for? I know it's not the beads."

My throat felt dry, and I could hardly swallow. "I'm looking for Darlene," I said quietly, "Have you seen her since she came in here yesterday?"

Donna grew solemn. "She was a wonderful person, wasn't she? We met a couple years back. She tested me at the municipal building. We would go out to dinner together sometimes; those were my favorite days. We talked about everything and everyone. We were as close as friends can get. But as time passed, we lost touch. We didn't talk again until yesterday, when she decided to check out my store."

I completely missed the fact that she was using the past tense. "Where is she?"

"She's gone!" Donna cried into her hands. "She's gone." She tried to gather her composure. "I told her to meet me at the La Sila mountain plateau. I told her I would be waiting for her. But she never came. And then there was a note. Darlene's sister gave it to me, because Darlene had told her that if she wasn't back by nightfall, then I should be given the letter."

Reaching under the counter, she slid it towards me, and I gave it a read. The letter said that Darlene had escaped Calabria somehow; she had wanted to leave so badly. Her whole life, she had been treated terribly by her family and even by random strangers. And it wasn't only that; she had been running from some things for a long time, and she had to leave. She said she had escaped via the Mediterranean and would hopefully arrive in America soon. Honestly, I felt like she'd be lucky just to make it to Spain; America was much too far away. Traveling all that distance from Italy to Spain solo on a boat seemed almost impossible. I didn't know how she would have been able to find the transportation and pull it off. The dictator could have her killed! The dangers of Darlene's escape made me begin to second-guess my own.

I began crying. I didn't know why I had liked Darlene so much so quickly; her delightful attitude was just so magnetic and pleasing. Why had she left when she had? Donna and I would have been there for her, I knew it. Maybe she had left because she couldn't be there for herself. I was in many ways similar to Darlene; I could never be there for myself when I needed it most. I wanted to support myself, but I also I wanted to have someone love me, and I tried so hard to love myself. But I couldn't, and I didn't even know why.

I dried my eyes as the thoughts of myself vanished. I focused on the thought that Darlene was likely dead. She had run away, just as I wanted to. What if I had gone with her? What would have happened then? Would I still be alive? I had wanted so badly to run away before. Would I risk it now, after what might have happened to Darlene?

I walked over to Donna and rested my head on her shoulder, and she rested hers on my head. We stood like that for quite a while, staring out the window. And I made a promise to myself that I would never forget that moment. I knew that Darlene could be looking down on us from Heaven, and she would be smiling. Everything would be okay.

Donna glanced at me with her weary eyes, lined with stress more than old age. She spoke in a fragile whisper. "I can help you," she murmured.

A shiver gently ran down my spine, and suddenly everything went cold. I wanted to talk to her, to ask her what she could help me with.

Instead, she was the one who broke the awkward silence. "You can leave—leave Calabria and all of your troubles behind. Maybe you can even meet up with Darlene."

I wanted to tell her that Darlene was dead, but I didn't really know if that was the truth. And I did want to join her; she was everything I aspired to be and more. I wanted to see her at least one more time. I had only known her for a short time—less than a day—but something about her and her personality was like a cup of warm cocoa, so inviting, whether on a winter's day or at dusk in late summer. Darlene was everything good, and everything bad. Maybe that's why I liked her.

Donna waited patiently for me to utter a single word. I didn't; I had not the slightest idea of what to say. There was silence for a while, and I wondered why she wouldn't just say something. She finally said in a quiet voice, "Go home, child. Get some good rest tonight. If you want my help, pack up all your essentials and come back here in the morning. I'll find a spare fishing boat. You'll leave the next day. Is everything clear for you, darling?"

I shook my head. My stomach was aching, and my head felt as if there were thousands of bees swarming around in it. There was buzzing, and the world got blurry. Everything was spinning. My hands got all sweaty and clammy, and it took a lot of effort to breathe. I realized I was dehydrated, and my mouth tasted salty, like I had just drunk seawater. I held my hands to my stomach as the ache grew worse. My throat felt hot.

Donna looked startled and asked if I was alright. I shook my head—and then vomited. I couldn't stop crying. Why couldn't I stop crying? My painful emotions washed over me before I lost feeling altogether. Everything morphed in odd ways as I slipped into unconsciousness. Colors swarmed around me in unfamiliar shapes, and I could still hear a weird buzzing sound, but that was all I remembered.

My eyes fluttered open, and I was staring at a white ceiling. I had no idea where I was; I was too tired to sit up and take in my surroundings. Instead, I fell asleep with the moon staining my face through the window with its silvery glow. I had completely forgotten about the fact that I was supposed to meet back up with Fleur for the cure. But I was too drained now, so instead I dreamed of joyous things, of a false reality.

SIERRA

Early morning. The smell of peaches and cream.

Wait… That was just a dream.

I crouched by my window once again, the sky dull and gray. It was the day of my soulmate testing. But there was honestly no need to show up; my presence there would mean nothing, at least in my mind.

My dad wasn't around. He worked in a corporate office. When people got married, their names were removed from the soulmate testing system, which meant that when men married, they could stop working. So, in the past, many boys had married at a young age so they could drop out of the system. Thus, Fleur had passed a new law: you could only get married after age thirty. When my mother had passed, my father had to return to work again.

For some reason, all I could think about was being an Angel. I wanted it so desperately. I couldn't stop thinking about the life I could've had. The Angels really didn't know how lucky they were; they took everything for granted. But one day, when the Earth stopped spinning, everything they owned would disappear. Would they learn their lesson then?

After a while, I simply brushed away my tangled thoughts and took a step outside into the salty seaside air to begin the walk from my house to the municipal building. At least the sun was shining. The moon was still visible, but a quarter of it was hidden.

I had only moved here two years ago from the western part of Calabria, which was currently home to the wealthier families. My father couldn't afford the rent on our old property, so we had taken everything we owned and brought it here, to the east side of Calabria. We'd had to start over again. Even though we only moved a few hundred miles, the weather and temperature had changed severely, because we had also traveled further south. I was still getting used to this climate, but today's weather made it much easier to transition.

No one was out today, apart from the rare passerby and the shopkeepers. The quiet was somehow deafening. I would usually long for quiet, as silence was what kept me thriving. But now all I wanted was to be surrounded by the comfort of people, even if they were strangers. The sensation of knowing someone was right beside you was perhaps one of the most reassuring feelings of all. My hood was pulled down tightly, covering most of my vision. I kept to myself as I wandered down the winding roads. I had walked about five blocks, which meant the municipal building would be in sight very soon.

I remembered a few years ago, when my father had gotten on his bike and picked me up as if I were six years old again. He placed me on his lap and kissed me on the head. I had frowned and instead situated myself in the old toy wagon attached to the bike. I recalled sitting there uncomfortably, but I thought anything was better than sitting in my father's lap like I was a baby. My father had started pedaling without saying a word, and we began the journey to the outdoor vendors in an awkward, uncomfortable silence. Looking back, I wished I had just stayed put on his lap. Now he was at work when I really needed him the most. The sky began to turn a muddy gray, and little droplets of water began falling. Perhaps the world was crying for me.

I finally arrived at the municipal building, and my feet were sore, the throbbing only increasing by the time I entered. I glanced at the informational plaque for a second I stepped into the elevator. It was spacious, and there must've been room for fifteen people, but I was alone. The walls, floor, and ceiling of the elevator were all glass, and as I traveled up to the second floor, I watched as everything below receded. The elevator doors opened to reveal a rather elegant lobby, more luxurious than the one on the first floor. I made myself comfortable on a velvet chair and studied the grime under my fingernails as I waited for the lines at the booths to shorten. But surprisingly, the lines only grew longer, and finally as the crowd reached the entrance, I realized I should've stepped into the line sooner. Usually, it was required for people to wait in a chair until called up to a booth. But there were apparently lots of people with the same birthday as mine, so the booths were accepting everyone, first come, first served. I waited for my turn at the end of the line and hoped that it wouldn't take all day; I didn't have that kind of patience. Maybe my mother hadn't either; maybe that was why she'd left this world so early.

Finally, an elderly woman with a tense posture and a taut bun ushered me forward, without any enthusiasm, a dull expression plastered over her face. I eagerly rushed up to her, not because I was excited, but because I wanted to get things over with. The woman had a golden badge pinned to her shirt: FRANCESCA. Francesca had blue eyes. Her face was very pale; it must have lost color over the years. Her hair was shoulder-length and chalk white.

Francesca began the process of signing me in. She asked for any form of identification I had on me. All people who entered the building for municipal business were required to bring an ID—a passport, driver's license, student ID, etc. I handed her my passport, which was empty, because I had never traveled anywhere. Francesca grabbed it from me without a word. Like most people who worked in this sad building on Giulio Camuzzoni Street, she was passionless, cold-blooded, and restrained.

Francesca led me down a long hallway to room 9 in the very back. The room contained a strange reclining chair and an even stranger machine. She spoke in a raspy voice, yet each word was enunciated. "I'll be staying in this room with you. Strict orders from the dictator. Sit in the reclining chair. I won't be asking you any questions today; we don't have the time." There was a sense of urgency in her tone. I didn't mind. She didn't procrastinate or stall one bit; everything she did was coordinated and efficient.

I obeyed Francesca only because I wanted to get everything over with. I quickly sat in the reclining chair, which was reminiscent of being in a dentist's office. Francesca mumbled some words under her breath that I couldn't understand. I eyed her as she began the challenging task of starting the machine and downloading all of its information. The machine was made in such a way that when you started it, you had to reload all the previously stored information on the other people and their test results, and then match it with your results.

Francesca waved her wrinkled hand and called out in a hollow voice that paired with her sunken eyes, "Help, please? The machine doesn't seem to be cooperating."

A man entered the room. He was bald, with hints of stubble sticking out here and there. He seemed kind and humble. I didn't know him—I barely knew anybody in this world—but I could read faces. I didn't have much of an education, so it wasn't books I was best at reading, but people.

The bald man was now talking in a thick accent that I couldn't correctly identify. "My name's Lamonte." He held his hand out and stood patiently as he waited for Francesca to shake it. She didn't. He awkwardly pulled his hand away and asked her what she needed help with. She crossed her arms over her chest and simply pointed to the machine as if she were merely a toddler, helpless and mute.

He took a deep breath and spoke in a crystal-clear voice, as if to make sure the elderly woman would hear. "I need you to tell me what the problem is with the machine."

Francesca frowned and tucked a dangling strand of white hair behind her ear. She spoke in a fragile voice that sounded as if it would break any second. "You're the tech guy. This isn't my job. Figure it out before I make a complaint."

I could see the urge in Lamonte's eyes to say something, to fight back. Instead, he calmly gathered himself and silently focused his attention.

After a while of just sitting in the tan recliner while he worked, I poked him in the back. He looked over his shoulder and stared at me with a bewildered and disoriented expression.

"You should've told her not to be so rude to you. She would've apologized," I whispered, half-hoping Francesca would hear me.

"Listen, I'm used to it. I don't want to lose my job. It's really not a big deal," he deferred.

"No, *you* listen. I'm old enough to know about inequality. I see it all the time in our society. There's gender and economic inequality everywhere; it's what Calabria thrives on. And the way that cruel woman just acted towards you was racially insensitive."

He shrugged. "Just because she's white and I'm black doesn't mean anything."

I sighed. "People have fought so long to end racism—millions of protests and marches and rallies. We're in the twenty-fourth century now, and it still isn't over. If we don't do anything about it, it's gonna live on until the sun explodes."

"But…"

"Just talk to her."

"I don't even know why I'm listening to you," he groaned. But then he walked over to the elderly woman where she was impatiently waiting for him to finish up, and he complained to her about her childish behavior. Francesca refused to believe she was wrong and pushed the man away. He gave up and returned to the machine. I smacked my hand to my forehead, and I knew he felt the same way. I didn't say anything after that, just silently sat there, patiently waiting for the machine's dilemma to be resolved.

The man rubbed his palms together repeatedly as he stood back and admired his hard work. Then he left without saying a word. Why should he? He was just the IT guy, after all, and I was a Devil. Perhaps that was why Francesca was treating me so horribly. I glanced at her enviously, loathing the elegant strands of pearls placed delicately around her neck. It was everything I'd never had, and so much more.

Francesa clasped her hands around her pearl necklace defensively, having seen my covetous glances. She wanted to protect such a priceless object from a Devil like myself. She spoke in a low whisper. "Let's get to it then, shall we?" Not knowing what else to do or say, I nodded. She continued, "Sit back in the recliner. We've already lost a precious half hour. I'll start by using the mind-scanning device."

My eyes widened at this. I did not want a random person whom I barely knew to scrutinize my personal thoughts.

Francesca spoke again. "Here, put these on. The goggles will allow you to designate which moments of your life I can view. These moments must be of great significance to you. Over fifty percent of your soulmate test results will be based on this."

I nodded with hesitation, and Francesca handed me the pair of goggles, which were similar to a virtual reality headset. The straps were well attached and stayed in place. She smiled and tapped several buttons on the screen before giving me her absolute attention. "This is my favorite part of working here," she confessed. "It's probably what has kept me at this job for over thirty years. Whenever you're ready, I'd like you to use your utmost concentration and focus in the center of your brain. Forget everything else. Just focus on your most predominant problems, and your most inspiring dreams. Leave everything else behind."

Francesca's voice calmed me, somehow so tranquil that it was the only thing I could think about. I attempted to focus, but it was hard with everything going on in my life. I tried to think about me having to hunt for water and food each and every day because of our scarcity. I tried to think about my late mother. I tried to think about wanting to become an Angel, about wanting to be of some significance. I thought about the house I grew up in before we moved. I tried to think of other specific moments and anecdotes, but it was hard. How about just yesterday, when I'd spent my sixteenth birthday alone, eating tiny bits of a cake? What about all the times when laughter was just a dream? What about the time when my own tears put me to sleep every night? It was painful to look back through almost every single moment in my brain and in my life. It hurt. For me, mental pain would always be worse than physical.

My thoughts were frayed and split. I tried to unite my memories and everything that had ever crossed my mind. There was so much pain, so much hurt. I couldn't bear it. Everything was too much—too much pressure, too many struggles, too many regrets, too much guilt, too much sorrow, too many tears.

But there was happiness too, hiding in unlikely places. I remembered dancing through a field dappled with sunflowers somewhere in eastern Calabria, the sun shining on my face and the breeze ruffling the strands of my dark hair. I had been foraging for food, walking for miles—and then I saw the flowers.

The sunflowers had danced with me, waltzed with me. Then there was that time when I had made a friend. Her name was Ember, and she was kind and gentle. We laughed together until our stomachs hurt. She was a soul I would have made great sacrifices for. I loved her. I missed her. And then I recalled a time when my father had given me a gorgeous silver necklace. I had almost cried, realizing that I was worthy of such a precious gift.

Suddenly, I removed the goggles, afraid that I had revealed too much. My eyes hurt; I wasn't used to the artificial light coming from them. Then I noticed tears forming in Francesca's eyes, and this surprised me, as she didn't seem like a very emotional person. I would never have thought she had the capacity to cry.

Francesca spoke to me through the tears. "I didn't know that you'd been through so much," she said. I nodded slightly, trying to conceal my somberness behind a thin veil. Finally, someone who had sympathy for me. She continued, "You seem to have picked out some good memories."

She waited for me to say something. I didn't. Finally, it was she who broke the silence. "We have a couple more things to do before you get your results. You should receive them around midnight tonight. You won't be receiving them in the gathering circle, because it's now under construction, so you'll have to come and find me right here in the municipal building before three a.m. at the latest. I would ask you to come in tomorrow morning, but we're on a very tight schedule, understood? And we need your full cooperation to be able to find you your soulmate."

I nodded once again, as my throat was too parched for me to speak. I had swallowed my tears, trying to hold them back, but it was a losing battle. I was also quite surprised that the gathering circle was under construction; the last time that had happened was probably in the nineteen hundreds. The gathering circle was a formal meeting place; it consisted of hundreds of curved stone benches that got smaller and smaller as they reached the center. On certain days, thousands of Calabrian residents would gather there in small groups to discuss any news or gossip. This was the only way that news traveled, as we didn't have the technology to share it. Dictator Fleur would also use the location to broadcast any new laws or restrictions that she was enacting.

Even on the days when Fleur didn't declare a gathering, the residents of Calabria would assemble there anyway. The kids would play in the field next to the stone benches. The adults would mingle, whether Devils or Angels. The rich would sip expensive wines, while the less fortunate would feast on any meat they could hunt. There was laughter, and people would sing songs and dance. My father and I used to go there, once upon a time. But that was a long time ago. We too would fill our bellies with any leftovers we could find, and after that, we would join in with the singing and dancing. Fleur knew this was happening, but she never stopped us from congregating in the gathering circle. She surprised me in that way.

In the summer, we would have barbecues. We went full-out with checkered picnic blankets, condiments, grilling utensils, and cups of all kinds of puddings and Jell-O. There would be smiles and laughter, and we would have these family-friendly gatherings almost every single day. For a while, all the stress in our little region would ease. The gatherings were something everybody could look forward to at the end of a long day. For the first time in a long time, Calabrians had something that made our culture so very unique.

My dad had told me to pack up immediately if Fleur ever came, so she wouldn't catch us having fun. I did see her once though, underneath a sycamore tree while everyone else was busy laughing, partying, and dancing. I saw her smiling with us. She didn't bother to stop our joy, which I thought was interesting. In reality, I realized, I knew nothing about her. She was kind, but she was cruel. She was pretty, but she was ugly. She was happy, but she was sad. She was neither bad nor good; she was both. She was this complicated paradox that no one could seem to figure out.

Francesca spoke again, snapping me out of my reverie. "The next task I would like you to perform is quite simple, at least in my opinion. I want you to stare at this painting intensely. What do you see?"

She held up a painting composed of hand-painted swirls in many vivid colors. On the base were swirls of teal, chartreuse, emerald, and royal blue. The middle of the painting had swirls of coronation pink and neutral corals. The top was painted with a sand-like texture. And then I saw it. At the bottom were the swirls of an ocean, dark waves tipped with white, like the foam that skimmed your feet when you stood at the edge of the sea. The middle of the painting encapsulated a rose-colored sky. Other colors like muted clay and della Robbia blue were painted across the sky, clearly by the hand of an experienced artist. I started to whisper uncertainly as Francesca too stared at the painting. She shushed me and pulled out an index card from the back pocket of her jeans. She then gestured for me to speak and stared closely at the card.

"I see an ocean," I said.

She rolled her eyes in an obnoxious way. "I'm gonna need more than that. Is it a calm or stormy ocean? What tells you that? What do the white specks symbolize? What do the pops of pink and orange mean? What does the change in the pattern convey where there are streaks instead of swirls? What does the sandy texture at the top of the painting express? We need more information to be able to match you with your soulmate. Is that clear?"

"Crystal." I took a deep breath. "The ocean—it scares me. There are monstrous waves that tower high. And the breeze… I imagine it smacking me in the face and tossing me into the deadly sea, and then the water pulls me under, and I can no longer breathe. I can still see the sky above me, and the clouds are getting smaller and smaller as I sink farther and farther down. I can feel the texture of the sand crumbling beneath me. I see sandstorms that swirl like mini tornadoes above my head, just as torturous. But beyond that, I see my life. This painting—it isn't art. It's me, my life. The ocean started out calm, but something happened, and it got rough and swirly and took me down with it. Where did that calm water go? Why is everything so hard?"

I abruptly snapped my mouth shut. I had said far too much, more than I intended. Francesca didn't move a muscle, just stared into the distance solemnly. Her voice trembled as she murmured under her breath, "I'm sorry."

"I don't need your pity," I said defensively.

"Well then, I appreciate you going into much more detail. This test is over. Remember to come back here to collect your results tonight after midnight. Okay, darling?"

I nodded and left without a single word. I took the long journey home, past Giulio Camuzzoni Street and towards the river, by the cliffs' edge. I didn't know why I preferred to take the longer route so much—perhaps because it was gorgeous and had such an aesthetically pleasing atmosphere. The cliffs were towers of large gray rocks that smelled of brine. The edges were sharp and hid many small cracks and crevices. The cliffs almost seemed to protect the river. The rippling water cared for the many fish within it, just as the cliffs cared for the river. It was like a carefully crafted watercolor painting, splashed with algae greens and vivid blues. The river was like a beautiful mirror, reflecting the sky above.

I would have loved to stay, but I had to go home. My father would be waiting for me. I kicked myself for taking the long route home. The view was nice, but it was getting dark, and then it would be the time of the thieves. The thieves came out almost every day in the late afternoon. Most thieves were Devils, trying to provide for their families. They would take anything they found from anyone they encountered. Devils had to do whatever they could to survive.

ANGELEE

I inexplicably woke up in my own bed. Morning already? Where had dusk gone? Where were the stars and their light?

It was gloomy again. My mother and father were talking loudly. It didn't seem like they were fighting, but I could sense the urgency in their tense voices. I panicked. Surely they had seen me by now. They knew I was still Angelee, right? I still had Angelee in me, I reassured myself. But I was also Fleur—a younger version of her. I didn't feel like a villain. In fact, I was everything but that—confident, determined, and brave.

It was raining again. I didn't mind it; rain evoked emotion, quite similar to the ones I was feeling at the moment. I walked to the kitchen. My mother and father were still speaking in worried voices, but I didn't know where they were. I watched as a blood orange rolled off the table and fell on the floor; someone must have just placed it there. I wasn't hungry, which was a good thing, because I definitely didn't want that floor orange. My parents' voices were getting fainter. They weren't going far, and they were pretending that everything was okay. It wasn't. Would it ever be?

As my mother entered the room and slid into the chair beside me, I didn't dare speak. Father came in soon after that, neither frowning nor smiling. He slid into a chair one away from mother. It was clear they were aggravated with each other. He plucked the orange off the floor and peeled it with an intense look in his eyes.

My mother sighed, then glared in my father's direction and hollered, "Am I the one who's supposed to tell her everything?!"

"Look, Carmella, I'm not saying that you should be the one to tell her everything." He took a deep breath. "All I think is that it would be better in this scenario if you explained our plans to her. Darling, please? You're better at this kind of stuff than me."

Carmella chuckled melodically. "Fine, if you insist." She turned to face me, and suddenly her pupils were bigger, and the fun side of her became more composed. She whispered gently, "You were out, cold, for twenty-four hours! And on top of that sweetie, you realize you're Fleur?" It seemed to be a rhetorical question, because she didn't wait for an answer. "Donna notified us that you had passed out in her shop. She had a letter personally delivered to us, and quite quickly at that. We came to pick you up and brought you home straightaway. When we saw you, at first we thought there was some mistake, that it wasn't you at all. But when we took a closer look, we realized you had somehow become a younger Fleur."

"So, you know everything?" I whispered back.

My mother nodded solemnly. "Donna did a wonderful job of explaining everything to us. I am so sorry you had to go through all that without us." She caressed my shoulder.

I instantly brushed her hand away. "I'm used to it," I snapped.

The room grew colder. My mother bit her lip furiously, and my father simply did nothing. Then my mother slammed her hands down on the table. "Do you not care about our family?! I wanted today to be a good day; that's all I wanted. I prayed to God it would be a good day. I guess that didn't work. I'm the only one who's putting in any effort around here! You don't care about either of us anymore—not your father, and not me." Tears rolled down her cheeks, but she looked as if she didn't even have the energy to cry.

My father's posture stiffened, and he was about to return to his room when he paused and spoke almost inaudibly. "Carmella, please. Please just calm down. We all need a break. Life has been busy. I think we should get away."

"Marchello, *you* calm down! Before we think about going anywhere, we have to get that blue serum from Fleur. And anyways, Calabria is useless now. Calabria is boring. There's nothing new here."

"We may think of Calabria as pointless, but that's only because of the dictator who governs it. Calabria is beautiful in itself. And yes, we'll get the blue medicine."

I paused and finally asked the question that had been haunting me most. "What about my soulmate?"

Mother and Father exchanged worried glances. Mother was the first to speak. "Let's not worry about that right now. There's honestly nothing to be anxious about. Getting that serum matters more than your soulmate. We can request a later time for you to head to go pick up your results. I think a breather might be nice. A lot has happened in the span of only a couple days, and it's completely natural if we all need some time to process everything that's been going on. I agree with your father: we need a break."

"It'll be like taking a road trip, but with no set destination," my father added. "Your mother and I can't do much research without access to the internet, of course, but we'll go old-fashioned and check out some brochures and newspaper articles. Is that okay, angel?"

My father called me "angel." It had nothing to do with wealth, abundance, or Heaven. It meant he loved me, and that was really it.

I uttered softly, "I think that might be good. It's what we need, and we haven't left our house in such a long time.

Soon after, I yanked a brown leather-bound suitcase out of the closet. My mother was doing the same, except hers was a faint green. I had a lot of clothes to choose from while packing—far more than I needed. We had factories that supplied all the clothes in Calabria, because they couldn't be shipped in or out of our region. The Angels owned the factories, and therefore, they were the only ones that could purchase the clothes.

I felt my mother's stare tickling the back of my neck. It was weird; I liked my mother, but I just didn't want to be near her right now. If you looked at the big picture, my mother wasn't all bad. She was the person who had fallen in love with me, but I was still learning to love her. She was the person who had adopted me, but I had ignored her many times. She was the person who provided for me, and I gave her nothing in return. Once I realized that, our relationship had begun to improve.

My mother reminded me of the sun covered by the mist that drifted through our vineyard. I didn't spend much time there now, but when I was little, it had been my favorite hideaway. The grapevines were a pretty green, and the grapes growing on them were pink and purple. Everything looked like I was stepping into a canvas, merging with the painting. And in early summer, mother would stuff the leaves of the grapevines for dinner.

Aside from being preoccupied with the work piling up and their busy job schedules, my mother and father also had to tend to the vineyard every other day. Adjacent to the vineyard was a factory where red wines were made, full of huge metal tubes and vats of grapes. The grapes themselves were good, rather bitter, yet the sweetness and acidity balanced out the flavors. I remembered last year, when I had tasted the first grape of the harvest. It was sweet, tangy, and bitter. I had smiled and closed my eyes to relish each and every second before it was gone. I was like that sometimes; I had to capture each moment in a memory, because it would never come back again. So, I took care to absorb the color of the sky and the clouds, the weather and temperature, the people with me and what they were saying, the setting and the atmosphere, the mood and emotions filling the room. I remembered wishing the taste of the grape would linger in my mouth for just one more moment, and I would be thankful.

Mother quietly went downstairs. She barely made a sound, so it was a while before I realized that she was gone. Then I could hear the muffled sound of my parents yelling at each other. I sighed, walked to my room, and closed the door.

I distracted myself from the weight of the world by looking at myself carefully in the mirror. The younger version of Fleur was quite pretty, with tousled honey hair highlighted with strands of strawberry blonde. My complexion was smooth and soft, and I smelled of vanilla extract. My nose and mouth were the perfect size, not too small or too big.

When I had seen Fleur back in the bead shop with Darlene, her eyes were bloodshot. But as I looked in the mirror now, they were a mix of blue and green. Her eyes were almond-shaped, icy and piercing, yet innocent somehow, sympathetic and sincere. Her eyelashes were long and thick. Fleur was pretty. But every time I saw her face in the mirror, the desire to become myself again became even greater. I wanted to see my own reflection. I wanted to cry like me, smile like me, laugh like me, scream like me. It hurt to be someone else; it only made me yearn to be myself even more.

I had not even the slightest idea of what my parents thought about this "new me." They must have been frightened when they looked into my eyes and didn't see their angel anymore. Come to think of it, my mother and father were probably hollering about *me*. But why would they waste their breath and valuable time on me?

Finally, there was silence. Thank God. I could still hear faint crying and sniffles, but I didn't care anymore. I used to cry about it; I used to cry when others would cry. But what did it matter anymore? I had spent my whole life caring about everybody else's well-being and had never taken any time for myself.

My mother soon walked back up the stairs, her cheeks tear-stained, her breath shaky. Even if she seemed like a villain sometimes, one of her traits that I had a fondness for was that she could read people so well. When she stared into your eyes, it felt probing, like she could see your deepest, darkest secrets. She could read into you, read your mind and body. And right now, she could tell I needed my space. My mother solemnly nodded and walked away.

It was quiet as she left, but once she reached her room, I could hear her softly humming a delicate tune—the one she had ever so gracefully sung to me as a baby. The song had been passed down through the centuries, from generation to generation. She had once explained to me that her great-great-great-grandmother, who had lived around the third millennium, had heard the song from her older sister.

The sisters had sat by the light of the moon in their bedroom, on a small bed that just barely fit the two. There were no curtains, which allowed the moonlight to pour directly in through the huge bay window. On every wall were miniature black-and-white photos of the children, their father, and their mother. A silver tray sat on the makeshift nightstand, holding petite sandwiches, mini raspberry scones, coffee cakes, and caramel candies. The elder sister, Jiera, reached for an apricot jam sandwich and began humming the same tune that mother would hum to me. The younger sister, Ela, had never heard this sweet sound before, and she asked curiously about what it was. Jiera explained that the melody had been written by their mother, before she passed. Their mother had been an opera singer, and people came from far and wide just to listen to her voice. She had loved music with all her heart and put her soul into it.

"The song I was humming," Jiera explained, "was something Mother made up once, long ago. That's the only thing I truly remember about her. She used to sing it to me every night before she tucked me in, and it soothed me so much. It was comforting. Now I'm singing it to you, and you must promise to pass it down to future generations, okay?" Ela had nodded firmly and smiled gently.

So, when I heard my mother humming the song, I knew I had to apologize for brushing her hand away earlier. I hadn't just brushed her away, but also her past and everything she was made of. I silently clung to the stair railing and closed my eyes. I walked on like that until I reached her bedroom. There were no lights on, and a thick fog embraced the sky outside. The only light came from the windows, but there was little sun, only gray. I could hear slight sniffles, and it made me want to break down as well.

I knew she would be in the bathroom, so that's where I went first. My knuckles rapped gently on the bathroom door. There was no response. My mother was probably wiping away her tears. I wanted her to know she didn't have to hide it anymore; I was old enough to understand.

I let myself into the bathroom silently. My mother was standing there clutching the windowsill, staring out into the vineyard. When I walked in, she gave no reaction. I didn't get discouraged, as this was the treatment I expected and deserved. I had to say something—but what should I say? I wasn't the best at opening up about my feelings, let alone talking to someone about their own. I wasn't about to give up though, since this was my fault, and all those days when I had thought of my mother as a villain were my own fault as well. Everything was always my fault.

She stiffened as I began speaking, and I could tell that my words struck her heart. They were uncomfortable, even for me.

"Mother, I'm sorry." Tears filled my eyes, except my tears weren't sweet; they were bitter. And even though it took so much courage and pain to say that to my mother, once it was out in the open, it hurt a lot less. Of course, I was terrified to see my mother's reaction, but I felt better than I had in a long time.

I stared at my mother, her facial expression incomprehensible. She was like a vacant void. I didn't expect her to speak, yet she did. I could barely make out her voice.

"I guess it's better now that it's out in the open," my mother said emotionlessly.

I couldn't tell if she was hurt or aggravated, so I just nodded. Then she murmured again, even more quietly, "Angelee, all I wanted was for you to love me. I thought you did love me. I thought you would give up anything for me, just like I would for you. And it hurts more than you think. What did I do that was so bad? I took you in like you were mine. Where would you be without me?"

I didn't say anything; I needed a few moments longer to process her words. Perhaps she wasn't waiting for an answer and merely wanted a hug or a token of my love. But I was too nervous to grant her wish.

She broke the silence. "Angelee, was I that bad? I tried to be there and provide for you. Did I not do enough for you? Please tell me. I just want to know everything I've done wrong."

Once again, I couldn't tell if she was upset with me or with herself. This time, however, Mother waited for me to say something, anything. But what could I say or do?

I remembered that when I was little, I had asked my mother what pressure was, and she explained to me that it was this feeling where you felt like you had to do everything, but inside you could do nothing. I felt that now. I wanted to apologize, except the words just wouldn't come out. My throat was burning, hot and heavy. My eyes were wet with tears, and I tried to wipe them away while my mother wasn't looking.

It felt like an hour before my mother finally said in a monotone voice, "Angelee, I really, really, love you, and all I hope is that you feel the same way about me, because from the moment I first looked in your eyes, I knew you would be forever mine. But I'm having doubts now, and I'm starting to believe that wasn't true, and it was all just a lie." My mother smoothed her skirt as she gathered herself and tried to keep her cool. Then she left the bathroom silently.

I collapsed into the bathtub, resting my elbows on my knees as tears streamed down my face. Sometimes I couldn't stop myself from crying. I knew you couldn't always be happy, and it was okay to cry every once in a while. Everyone did. At many times though, I wished to go somewhere else and be with somebody else. Maybe that person would be similar to me and my personality. I just wanted to find someone who could truly *get* me. I wanted someone to understand me without me having to explain. I just wanted someone to understand. I mean, didn't we all? Except everyone else had someone. I wanted someone too. Yes, I had my mother and father, but I wanted someone younger who was struggling just like me. Maybe once I received my soulmate test results, I would have a friend for life.

I would have loved to have a sister, to sit in our beautiful vineyard and laugh and share secrets. We could sit together at the cliffs by the edge of the blue sea. We could spend our days together— each and every one. We could share clothes and smiles, and just lie on our beds and chat about everything. I couldn't help thinking about how different my life would be if I had a friend in my life. I could start over again, and it wouldn't be as frightening or scary when I had someone by my side. Of course, we might get in fights sometimes, but that's life, and we all had our little disagreements. Things would be happy again, but only if I had a best friend, a soul sister. How I wished I had someone like her. Then maybe the rain would stop falling and the sun would start shining.

I continued crying as I sat in the bathtub. It was still foggy and rainy outside, and it appeared that the sun wouldn't come out for a while. I usually didn't mind the rain; it was calming. I could fall asleep listening to the steady pitter-patter of rain as it fell on the roof. But today, it just added to the miserable atmosphere.

I slowly stood up and exited the bathroom. Tears stained my cheeks, and I silently wiped them away. I stood at the top of the stairs, and I knew I should go down, but I was scared. I didn't know why, but I felt like once I got down there, I would be even more crushed. Mother was still upstairs, but my father was down below. It would be best to stay on this floor, because that's where my bedroom was. I would just have to sneak past my mother and try my best to avoid her. Even the slightest breath or movement could give me away. I tiptoed in the direction of my room and managed to get there in no time. I twisted my doorknob all the way to the left, so that when I closed it, it would make no sound.

An antique Italian chair sat in the corner of my room, decorated with floral patterns on soft white fabric. There were all kinds of flowers, but mostly cherry blossoms and chocolate cosmos. There were no thorns on any of the stems, and that comforted me. I had never paid much attention to the chair; it was just another object that had sat in my room for all these years. But it meant something to me; it was the only thing I owned that had belonged to my biological mother and father. I honestly didn't know why I never really sat in the chair, when it belonged to the person whom I was related to not only by blood, but also in my heart. I would have loved to meet my biological mother, and maybe if I sat in that chair, I would find a piece of her.

I dragged the chair across my room and pushed it up against my door, making sure no one could enter. Then I sat in the light of the sun peeking through. I had always wanted someone to be around when I was alone, but now that I *did* have someone around, I just wanted to be alone. I wished life, for once, could go my way. I wished that one day, all of my dreams would come true. Maybe then, everything would be okay.

There was a gentle knock on the door. I pushed my chair back to the corner of the room, but didn't let it touch the wall as it had before. If it was my mother who was knocking, I childishly wanted her to know I had been using the chair; maybe then she would feel the slightest hint of jealousy. I left the door partially ajar, and my mother sauntered into the room, accompanied by my father.

Why was she so tranquil now? Even though I said sorry, hadn't I just crushed her entire world? It should have soothed me that she wasn't struck by my words, but instead it pained me. I was frightened that she had taken it in such a relaxed manner. Maybe my apology *did* mean something to her. Both my mother's and father's moods were unpredictable. My mother obliviously took a seat in the floral chair I had just sat in. My face reddened. That was my mother's chair—my real mother, the one I truly loved!

My whole body was trembling, and I couldn't contain it anymore. I refused to be governed by these people who called themselves my parents, nor was I going to be their pitiful daughter anymore. While I had once looked up to them and done whatever they told me was right, I would no longer listen to their rules, nor obey their demands. It was all over.

Everything was gone. But where did it go? Where did everything go?

SIERRA

It was dark outside, but the moon shone bright. From where I was sitting by the large bay window, I could see the rich chartreuse hills where the Angels lived. It was late—11:00 p.m., to be exact. Dad had been held back at his job, forced to work until sunrise, at the earliest. So, it was just going to be me. To be honest, I was quite anxious about the results of my testing and who my soulmate would turn out to be. I was not at all like my mother; I would never be as courageous as she had been. I hadn't gotten my father's personality either; he was strong and bold, while I was timid and reserved.

My meal was hot cocoa that was actually cold and a piece of toast without butter. Some days I was lucky; my father would bring fresh fruit home from work and squeeze it into juice for dinner.

In the past, we'd had to get all our daily and weekly necessities shipped directly from Fleur. We would fill out a form each Sunday and write down what we would need for the week: eggs, a gallon of milk, rye bread, two tomatoes, one container of dish detergent. That was all we could afford, nothing more. But now that the shops and cafés were open, we didn't have to worry about filling out that stupid form anymore. But at the same time, we didn't even have a quarter of the food the Angels had, or enough money to buy food throughout the scorching summer.

I had to forage for food a lot of the time. Those were the hardest days. Of course, only a few days that I particularly remembered could be called enjoyable, and that was when I had time for myself or when I came home early from foraging. But all those things happened rarely.

I was thoroughly cherishing my dinner, as I didn't have it too often. Though the hot cocoa wasn't hot, it was still comforting on a mild summer day. And even though the toast wasn't buttered, it was still good enough for me—much better than nothing.

I packed my backpack for the long walk to the municipal building. My father didn't want me to go alone, but unfortunately he had to work, and none of our neighbors were available to accompany me. I was left all by myself. I brought some leftover toast in a used bag, a sweatshirt (the only one I owned), as the nights were rather cold near the sea, and a pocketknife that had belonged to my mother's mother. I slipped on a pair of cozy woolen socks and made sure to lock the door of our apartment as I departed.

I was never one to talk about our home, not even during my few years in school. It was small and humble: my room, my father's, a washroom, and a kitchen, with nothing more than the essentials. We didn't even technically have a living room. We relied on a few necessary items to keep us thriving, which included a fully functioning toilet and sink. I didn't spend much time in our small apartment anyway. I was mostly outside, either in the woods behind our property, or in the lush hills that rolled for several miles before becoming flat again.

When I was little, I would play with my imaginary friend, or sometimes with my only real one, whom I would meet up with after school. We would spend countless hours exploring what nature had to offer. We would roll down the hills to the old abandoned barn that nobody had been in for years. We would hike in the woods and examine fascinating creatures. We would play hide-and-seek and conceal ourselves in the cover the woods provided. In the winter, we would run to the frozen creek and find sticks to poke and prod each piece of ice before we made sure it was stable enough to walk on. Sometimes we would just take long walks and talk for hours, eating sweet tangerines that we delicately picked off the tall trees. My friend didn't have a mother, and our dads were at work, so it was mostly just the two of us.

But now my friend was gone, one day she simply stopped coming to the hills, and I felt quite lonely. I was too old to play with my imaginary friends anymore. So, I rolled down the hill by myself and made a promise never to go inside the barn. I hiked through the woods by myself, but was too scared to examine the bugs without the comforting presence of my friend. I walked along the creek's edge by myself. I ate the tangerines by myself, only they didn't taste sweet anymore. She had been my best friend. She was like a sister to me, but then in a flash, she was gone. Now I had lost both my best friend and my mother.

I continued walking along the winding, half-paved sidewalks that made up our neighborhood. It was like living past nights all over again. The trees swayed gently in the wind. No one was around. I wasn't scared; I liked the quiet. It was used to it. It was familiar. Scraggly bushes lined the paths I was walking on. The moon hung high, an almost perfect crescent. Occasionally, I heard distant sounds. Other than that, everything was quiet. It was haunting and gloomy, and all I had was myself for company.

My head was pounding with pointless thoughts. I knew my heart was supposed to be soaring, but I was scared and filled with anxiety. Did I even want a soulmate? Maybe. I wanted—a sister, or perhaps a brother. I wanted someone to look up to. I wanted someone to watch over me, laugh with me, and dance and sing with me. I wanted someone to cry with me, talk with me, and listen to me. I wanted someone to scream with me, hurt with me, heal with me. I wanted someone to *be* with me. I just wanted to have someone. I had my father, but he wasn't around much. And it wasn't that I didn't love him, because I did; it just wasn't the same. It was hard when someone wasn't there for half of your life. Of course, he had to support and provide for us. Still, I wished I had someone by my side.

There it was up ahead: the municipal building, standing broad and confident in the dead of night. I braced myself and took a deep breath before I headed up the cobblestone pathway to the familiar yet unfriendly building. Only dim lights could be seen from where I was standing. Fleur usually kept her employees working late, so the fact there were only a few lights on in the building was quite a surprise to me. I had half expected the soulmate testing center to be bustling and packed with people. Instead, there were no more than fifty people in the area.

I stepped into the building. Assorted varieties of flowers were arranged in bouquets that dotted the lobby and the first floor. I stepped into the elevator with its glass walls. No people were behind me, only me, going up and up. My stomach jumped. Then everything stopped, and the elevator doors opened.

I was greeted by dim lighting and a familiar woman standing at one of the only open booths. Francesca waved at me in a polite fashion. I forced a smile. I was no actress, and it was hard to fake something that wasn't real. I walked closer to her, so I could hear her whispered hush.

"Ah, Sierra. Thank you, darling, for coming at this hour. We had no other available time slots that would have been convenient. Why don't we end in the room where we started?"

I nodded stiffly, following Francesca down several long and narrow hallways. When we finally reached the room, I was greeted by pops of vivid color and a cold, hard bed frame. Francesca walked over to a small cupboard in the corner of the room, the tan paint chipping off. She opened it to reveal hundreds, maybe even thousands of miniature envelopes. I was guessing that the envelopes contained the results of each soulmate test. Francesca dipped her hand into the pile of scattered envelopes and took them out one by one. She scanned the names in the right corner of the envelope. Many times she shook her head while examining the data. It took ages, until finally she pulled out a stiff white envelope and scanned it before giving a pleased nod and tearing it open.

Francesca smiled wearily and asked in a quiet voice, "Are you ready?"

I nodded. There was no turning back now.

"Sierra, would you like me to read this? You could do the honors as well. After all, these are your results."

"Ugh," I groaned with as much effort as I had left inside of me. "I really have no choice, do I?"

She shook her head and handed me the letter with a smile plastered on her face. It was fake; I could tell. She must have lived through this scenario over and over again, too many times to count. She offered a choice, but the recipient always ended up reading the letter, and then she would pretend that everything was going to be okay, when in truth it wasn't. I really wanted someone like a brother or sister, yet it was awful that this system put so much pressure on us, the weak and the helpless, the desperate and the poor. I took a deep breath, scanning the pages before I read them. I carefully digested the information before I read it out loud to Francesca.

Soulmate Results

Dear Sierra Berlusconi,

We have carefully processed your answers from the various questions you were asked, your memories, and the painting exam. Your soulmate has been very cleverly chosen. You have been paired with Angelee Anand. You will find that being paired with another female is quite convenient. Enclosed, please find some additional information about her and her family that has been approved to share with you.

Address: 427 Via del Corso, Calabria, Italy

Family members: Carmella Anand (mother), Marchello Anand (father)

Background: Angelee Anand was born in Calabria. She was adopted by Marchello and Carmella when she was only a few weeks old.

Angelee's maternal grandparents originally immigrated to Italy from their home city of Mumbai, India. It was a long voyage, especially since Carmella was just a baby. Her parents gave Carmella an Italian name in honor of the place where they hoped to raise her. They tried to scrape together anything they could and sold all their precious belongings. Sometimes they had to go days without eating.

When she got older, Carmella worked hard every day to help out her parents. She eventually settled down and married her husband, Marchello. Then they adopted Angelee, and they started a life of their own, eventually becoming very successful in their careers.

Angelee grew up to be kindhearted. She had everything she could want, but she didn't have the loving support of her adoptive parents. The price of their wealth and power was constant work, leaving their daughter on her own much of the time. While your backgrounds are very different, Angelee truly does have the heart of an Angel.

Francesca shook her head thoughtfully. "That's all, kid? They don't even tell us her ranking. How are we supposed to know if she's an Angel or a Devil?"

"Oh, Francesca, isn't it obvious?. There's so much evidence in the letter. Look at her name: *Angel*-ee! And it says her parents are powerful and wealthy, and she grew up wanting for nothing! It's quite clear that she practically owns the world!"

With this, Francesca looked at me in a disoriented way. And that's when it truly sunk in that my soulmate was an Angel, and I was a Devil.

I rushed out of the room, Francesca calling after me. I tried to find my way through the maze of hallways until I was out of breath, my heart pounding. I had thought that Devils couldn't be paired with Angels. Did that mean I was really an Angel, or she was really a Devil? I couldn't take it anymore; everything was just so overwhelming. Suddenly a weight was crushing me, and I could barely keep moving.

When I finally found the second-floor lobby, I spotted a woman with thick black box braids that tugged the roots of her hair. I rushed up to her booth. "Ma'am!" I was nearly yelling at this point. "I think the system has made a mistake! I'm paired with an Angel, and I'm nothing but a Devil!"

The woman shrugged, seeming nonchalant. She muttered in a monotone voice, "Darling, didn't Francesca notify you about our new system? We've made several colossal changes that will truly impact Calabria's lifestyle, as well as yours. First of all, men will only be paired with men from now on. Same goes for women; they will only be paired with women. And yes, there's a reason behind this. We truly understand that while the men are out doing their work in the fields, women will be quite lonely. We wanted you to be paired with a soulmate who could be your best friend or sister. I hope this is clear?"

I didn't nod. It was stupid; it made no sense. What about the people who didn't identify with a specific gender? And she hadn't even answered my question.

"Okay, well, what are the other changes you've made to better your system?" I asked, hoping she would give me a real answer.

"That's classified. All I'm allowed to say is that Angels and Devils can now be paired. Fleur has changed. We've heard from her associates, as well as from her family. All of them say the same thing, and we've come up with a theory as to why she's been acting so different lately. It's as if her eyes have just been opened to the world she's governed for such a long time, like she's finally realized the reality of this world and the little region of Calabria. She finally sees the hardship that the Devils are facing every day. It's the first time she's cared for someone other than herself. She's clearly had a change of heart. Personally, I think she's seen something—perhaps read a certain book, or met certain people, or encountered an unhealthy situation. It's like the lens distorting her view of reality has finally come off."

I just nodded. "There's no mistake, then? I'm supposed to be paired with an Angel?"

The woman just gave a simple nod.

"So, where can I find my soulmate, Angelee?"

She looked at me, unsure. "We're not sure about Angelee's exact location right now, but we've already left a note for her on the front door of her mansion. Unfortunately, she hasn't responded yet, but we told her to meet you here at the municipal building. Maybe something came up."

She paused. "Actually, let me do a quick search right now. We just got these new computers; they can do almost anything. I can track her car through her licence plate. Hopefully she's in it right now."

The woman was quick on the computer and found my soulmate's location in no time.

"It seems that she's moving right now, and pretty quickly. Right now, she's at the intersection of Giulio Camuzzoni and Via Del Comune. If you hurry up, you might be able to catch her."

I nodded and sprinted away without a word. I was still just completely astonished that my soulmate was an Angel, and I was a Devil.

I exited the building and found myself on the deserted street. The moon was beaming bright, like thousands of fireflies, full and perfectly round. I could feel the rough cracks in the pavement through the worn soles of my shoes. If I stopped walking for a second, I could feel Calabria's heartbeat, alive with people, alive with sound, alive with beauty. It was unusually quiet though; the heartbeat was faint, with not much life in it. My own heart was beating in unison with the streets and the few people that were out. I scanned my surroundings. It was a long street that stretched over a few miles.

Mile one was soon completed; two more to go. Despite the regular exercise I got from hunting and foraging, my feet were aching on the unforgiving pavement. My heart was pounding, and each step I took was torture. My head was spinning and throbbing. I didn't know why everything hurt so much. Yet there was still something in my mind pushing me forward. It was like a Devil was sitting on my left shoulder, and on my right was an Angel, pushing me to turn back towards comfort and security. But I was a Devil at heart, and as I kept moving, the doubts eased.

One more mile until I reached the end of Giulio Camuzzoni Street. I tried to catch a glimpse of headlights glowing in the hazy fog and listened for the sound of a car. Nothing. There were no cars in sight. In fact, there were no people to be seen other than myself.

When I reached the end of the street, I sat down and just waited for a while. Finally, a woman emerged silently from the fog. I could only make out her silhouette in the dim glow of the streetlamps. I picked myself up from the musty pavement and walked closer, until my shadow was almost touching hers. She was walking a few feet ahead of me. I glanced at her reflection in the windows of the shops as we passed. She had bloodshot eyes, gleaming with a deadly poison. Her straw-textured hair wasn't as glowing and thick as it had been. Her lips were chapped, her eyelashes seemed sparse, and her nose was irregular. But what hadn't changed was her personality, for she was Dictator Fleur, and she was the magic that made Calabria thrive. Of course, she hurt Calabria in more ways than she healed it. I was only just beginning to realize that.

The dictator hadn't even noticed my presence, so I tapped her on the shoulder gently, so as not to frighten her. She swiftly spun around and stared me directly in the eyes. The ice in her gaze ran down my spine and made me shiver slightly. Yet she quickly softened, like butter in a heated pan. Her eyes turned warm, and so did her smile. Even her tone was consoling. "Yes, Sierra?"

I didn't even bother to ask her how she knew my name, but let her continue without interrupting.

"Are you in search of your soulmate? I believe her name is Angelee. She's aware that you're arriving. I tracked her location only moments ago via her parents car, and it seems she's stopped moving. It's possible that she's waiting for you. The only problem is that she stopped right by the port of Gioao Tauro, and there will be lots of people there. It's best that we take a car."

My heart completely stopped. I had never had the luxury of riding in a car. Most people in the region of Calabria didn't own cars, because Fleur considered it "a way out." Luckily, there were trackers on all of them. Devils could only dream about having a car, whereas Angels just needed to meet basic requirements to own one.

Fleur waited for me to respond, but all I did was nod. I obeyed the dictator's orders and followed her to her car. When I saw it, I had to admit that I hadn't expected Fleur's car to be quite so luxurious—unique, perhaps, but not in an opulent way. The car was a Bugatti Veyron, one of the most expensive and well-known brands in Italy. It must have cost Fleur a fortune to afford such a luxury. The sporty car embodied the sleek power of a jet, and for a few seconds, I actually believed that the car would take me up, up, and away. Fleur took the driver's seat on the right, and I took the passenger seat. The leather seat felt soft against the fabric of my thin blouse. Fleur inserted something into a slot, and the car started moving. The pace was slow and bumpy at first, but we accelerated in less than a few seconds. I couldn't help but grin, wishing the feeling of freedom and exhilaration would last forever. The windows miraculously opened with a single command, and the wind tousled my hair. I felt like a bird, free and happy.

I was free as a bird, but I had only just found my wings. I was sitting next to a dictator, but I still felt ungoverned. There was a stop sign ahead, but Fleur didn't bother to stop. She had power, and she knew how to use it.

ANGELEE

Everything was speeding by—the trees, the houses, the lights, the people. I couldn't really see anything except the occasional faint silhouette. The sky was black; I couldn't see the stars. My mother was driving, my father sitting in the passenger seat. I was stuck in the back seat.

Father spoke to me in a tense manner. "Aryan is on our way. He's staying at a small motel less than ten minutes from here. We could either get the formula now, or on the way back from our trip. Your choice."

Mother rolled her eyes. "There is absolutely no choice involved. We're getting the medicine now."

The motel looked pretty cheap, with tan walls, a black roof, and a giant neon-red sign that read, *Motel*. Aryan was already standing outside, arms crossed, glasses fogged due to the humidity. His hair was thin and graying. He wore a black V-neck T-shirt and oversized jeans that were loose around the waist, and a leather belt to prevent the jeans from slipping. His stubble was gradually starting to take over and form a mustache on his upper lip. His eyes were small, but their intensity was almost scary.

"I know you have somewhere to be, so we'll make this quick," Aryan said as we stepped out of the car. He handed me a glass mason jar containing a blue fluid. I guessed it would take more than just a spoonful to get me back to normal. The man instructed me to take slow sips; if I drank the formula too fast, it would be overpowering. My mother waited patiently for me to finish, while my father fidgeted with his fingers. Once I was done, Aryan spoke hastily to my parents, making sure to let us leave on time for our "mini excursion."

"Yes, so, I recommend that she come back here within seven days to receive the next dose," he said. "That should conclude the process, and she won't have to worry about it again"

"Alright, I just have a quick question," my mother said.

Aryan nodded. "Go for it."

"How long are you staying at this motel? We're really looking to get away, and my best guess is that we won't be back in seven days. I mean, this is my only chance to take a break from work this year, and I really want to enjoy it without worrying about the hassle of getting back here."

"Well, I specifically took this trip to provide you with the necessary medication, so I'll be staying here until Angelee is back to her ordinary self. Plus, I've never been to Calabria, and I wouldn't mind doing some exploring."

I tuned out what the adults were saying, plucking a dandelion puff from a crack in the parking lot. I blew on it, and the wind carried away the hundreds of tiny seeds. One after the other, they all dispersed into the darkness, with the hope of turning into something beautiful one day. I wished to escape Calabria, to leave everything behind. And I hoped that the dandelion seeds would bloom elsewhere, so that someone could appreciate their beauty just as much as I did.

"Thank you so much, Aryan."

I suppressed a grin. I rarely heard words of gratitude leave my mother's mouth. It seemed as if she felt forced to say it.

"It's no problem. Happy to help."

"We should be on our way now," my mother said. "We'll catch up with you later and most likely be here within ten days' time."

"That's fine. If anything changes, you know where to find me."

My mother gave a reassuring nod. She held my hand as we walked back toward the car. Yet, I could tell she was still scared of people seeing me on the streets. Everyone hated Fleur, and if anyone saw me "impersonating" her, it could ruin my parents' reputation as well.

Just then, I heard the faint sound of a distant engine. It sounded like it was coming from behind us. I peeked through the back window, trying to see past the piled-up luggage. A car, very similar to ours, was following us. My mother and father hadn't realized this; they could barely see in the rearview mirror because of all the suitcases we had crammed in the back. I looked closer. My eyes could barely make out the silhouettes inside. But whoever it was was up to something; I just knew it. I strained my eyes. Who was following us?

Weirdly, I honestly didn't even mind. I wasn't scared; in fact, I enjoyed the bit of excitement and drama. The sensation of the luxury engine was exhilarating. A rush of adrenaline and an urge to move ran through my body. I continued to watch the car as it came closer, now perfectly in view. I could finally see the people inside. On the passenger side was a girl I had never seen before, unrecognizable. She had charcoal-black hair down to her waist that looked darker than the velvety night sky. Her eyes were as round as the moon, framed by long lashes. Her smile was symmetrical, the shape of a tangerine slice. The shape of her face was more of an oval than a circle, and her cheekbones were well defined. Her expression gave the impression that she was kind and well mannered.

Sitting exactly next to her was a familiar woman, her face plastered with a fake smile. It could only be Fleur. *Great*, I thought to myself. *I always knew one of us would get executed, and this must be the day.*

I urged my mother to speed up. Automatically, she started to do so, then immediately slowed down. "Angelee, honey, why do we need to go faster?" she asked me softly, yet I could still make out the tension in her voice.

"Fleur is right behind us. She's on our tail, gaining on us!" With every word, the urgency in my tone increased.

My mother looked back at me anxiously in the rearview mirror. "Honey, are you sure? I don't want to speed; it's dangerous." She was driving at a crawl. Our luggage was blocking her view, so I was acting as a mirror for her.

"Mom!" I pleaded. "I'm not lying, I swear! Just please don't get us killed because you don't believe me!"

My mother took a deep breath and pulled off to the side of the road with a sudden lurch and a screech of tires. I smacked my palm against my forehead. Fleur and her sidekick would be on us any moment to break down everything we had built up. How was Mother simply letting these nightmares come to life? Father was whispering to her, but I could only hear snippets of the conversation.

Fleur's car came to a halt behind us. Fleur stepped out, and so did my mother and father. I stayed in our vehicle, and the girl in the passenger seat stayed in theirs. We made eye contact through the mass of luggage, and I quickly shifted mine away. That must have discouraged her; she didn't give me another glance.

My parents and Fleur were standing on the side of the street. I opened my door so I could hear.

"Yes, Angelee is definitely a wonderful girl." Mother was blowing her nose into a silk handkerchief with Fleur's initials embroidered on it in baby blue, half crying. "I don't know what I did wrong. She thinks of me as a villain."

"Trust me," Fleur responded, "I know what it feels like. Everyone's hating on you, and you feel so helpless, like you can't do anything about it. You want to fix the way people think of you. They keep thinking you're bad and evil. You make one mistake, and you get criticized for the rest of your life because of it. I did everything for my sister and my mother. I wanted them to look at me with approval. I really loved them, and I wanted to finish what they had started not so very long ago. My mother always said to write an ending for every story you start. I did it for both of them. I'm trying to help, but what am I doing wrong? I worked so hard to get where I am right now; you wouldn't even understand. In fact, you're amongst the lucky ones; only one person holds a grudge against you, and only barely. I have thousands that despise me. But don't worry, Angelee's soulmate will help heal her wounds, and Angelee will do the same for her in return, I imagine. It will all be okay. Just live in the moment without a single worry or fear. That's why I've brought Sierra here; she'll fix everything. Would you care to meet her?"

My mother seemed comforted by the dictator's sincerity. It was as if Fleur were gently singing her a lullaby. My mother nodded, and Fleur motioned for Sierra to come out of her silent trance and greet my parents. Sierra exited the car. Mother and Father greeted her with a firm handshake, and the girl gently waved at me with a polite grin. "Hello," she said confidently. She looked to be my age. And then I realized with astonishment, she was my soulmate. The girl I was looking at would be my friend, my sister.

Fleur bit her lip. My mother smiled uncertainly, but I could tell she was still unsure, and my father had some doubts as well.

"Hi, sweetie," my mother said. "Uh, how would you like to meet our daughter? I'm sure she would be very pleased to finally meet her soulmate. I'll let her introduce herself; we have some things to discuss with Fleur in private. I'm sure my daughter would be happy to take a stroll with you to one of the beaches, perhaps Scilla. We might take a while, so don't rush. But it was very nice to meet you. Sierra, right? One thing about me: I'm not good with names. Anyway, we'll talk more later." And with that, she turned back to Fleur.

Sierra nodded with utmost poise. As she approached the car, I saw my father rambling on, when he usually tended to stay quiet. Intrigued as I was by this mystery girl, I couldn't help but listen in.

"All I'm wondering is what economic group that girl comes from. I don't want my daughter hanging out with some Devil. I want to be sure that she'll be safe in the company of her soulmate, alright?"

It wasn't like my father to be so assertive. He was the geeky type of dad who always put on a front, so I was quite surprised. Fleur wasn't oddly, she seemed terror-stricken. It was the second time I had seen her so helpless and vulnerable. She usually kept herself above everyone else, like she was sitting on a throne while everyone else was down below her, wearing a shining jeweled crown while everyone else was reflected in it.

Fleur cleared her throat obnoxiously. Perhaps she was trying to clear the fear out of her body. "I'm afraid I can't tell you that."

"Listen, I can't take this anymore. It's really simple: just tell me her rank. I'm starting to think you're hiding something from me, and if my daughter is paired with this girl, I'd like to know everything about her immediately! This isn't a joke. I need answers, and I should have the privilege of receiving them from you!" he hollered.

The dictator looked close to tears, but she pushed them back. "Mr. Anand, I have dedicated my whole life to this," she said in a weak voice, yet it still contained so much intensity. "It's my fault. I feel so stupid sometimes. Everything I've ever done has been a lie. And it's my fault that people like you are turning into what you are."

To this, my father clearly took offense. But my mother quieted him down and signaled for Fleur to continue.

"Why did I even do this?" Fleur muttered despondently. "The soulmate system is alright for now, but the Angels and the Devils are too much. If you want the truth, I'll give it to you! Yes, Sierra is a Devil. But that doesn't mean she's a bad person. Doesn't she seem so kind? Aren't you impressed by her manners? Just because she's a Devil doesn't mean you have to hate her. She's just like you and me; she's just had fewer opportunities. I was dumb and blind before; I couldn't see. It's as if my eyes are suddenly open to the world. So, please don't judge her. This is all my fault. Please."

My mother and father both nodded in agreement. By now, Sierra was standing outside my window, her hands gripping her hips, yet her expression still seemed patient. My window was slightly cracked. I heard Sierra speak in a low voice intended for my ears. "You kind of look like Fleur."

Some greeting. "It's complicated, but at the soulmate testing, I pressed a button on the eye-scanning machine. Somehow, someway… I am now a younger version of Fleur. I already received a dose of medication earlier today to get me back to normal, but it takes a few hours to settle in. ," I sighed.

"Sorry, that was a terrible introduction. I'm Sierra. Your mother said we should take a walk to the beach. I know I'm a Devil and all, but maybe we can learn to get along."

"Sierra, you don't have to say that. It doesn't matter to me whether or not you're an Angel."

She smiled gratefully.

"And let's go to Scilla," I suggested. "I haven't been to the ocean in so long… In fact, that's why we were in the car: we were heading down to the beach to explore Calabria. We all just need a break from the world."

Sierra nodded and politely opened the back door for me. Mother waved to me with a gentle hand, and I waved back. She was smiling, and I knew she was making peace with this. Her eyes were finally opening as well.

Suddenly, Sierra took my hand and started sprinting, and I was running with her. I felt the earth as I ran. I felt the wind and the darkness. We kept on running all the way down the street.

Scilla looked like a scene from a movie with its picturesque yellow-and-white-striped umbrellas. Large boulders divided the beach into two separate sections. One of them was called Marina Grande, the section that most tourists had visited before Calabria became restricted to foreigners, because of its clear waters. The other section was called Chianalea, which had once been used as an old fishing port. Chianalea had beautiful houses that seemed stacked on top of one another, built directly upon the cliffs. Quaint alleyways and staircases accented the small beach town. The stairs led all the way up to the top of the rocky hill, from which you could get a clear view of the beach.

I hadn't been to the beach in forever. It looked endless. The shore went on for miles and miles, white sand that seemed to stretch into infinity. You couldn't tell where it started or ended. The water was shallow even a hundred feet in, and the currents and tides were mild. In winter, mist would hide the ocean horizon in a blanket of fog. My parents had told me that the beach looked ghostly without all the tourists.

When Sierra and I reached Scilla, I followed her through the dim lighting to the fishing port of Chianalea. Just like I remembered, crumbling houses were stacked upon each other on the jagged cliff. Sierra and I held hands as we made our way to the ocean. The sand was rough, with fragments of rocks and seashells everywhere. When one of us stumbled, we would hold on even tighter, until my hands were reddened.

There were many boats all lined up along a dock, and others floating in front of abandoned houses. The boats were rarely used, and Fleur had once planned to confiscate them, but the fishermen who caught wild bass still needed them for their jobs. After all, fresh-caught wild bass was Calabria's main export. In fact, Calabria was primarily known for fish. Because of our access to miles and miles of ocean, countries from all parts of the world would trade with us.

"So," Sierra murmured under her breath, "what should we do?"

"I don't know. I guess we could just turn back at this point," I said uncertainly.

Sierra reluctantly nodded. "We could, but we only just got here. These days, no one is allowed at the fishing port, so we should use it to our advantage."

I had to say yes to that. "Okay, why don't we sit in one of those boats over there?" I walked with her along the shore, moving carefully so I wouldn't stumble on the rocks.

Most of the boats were fishing boats that ranged in size, but some were larger vessels used for charter cruises. The fishing boat that I was staring at had a sturdy deck made of wooden planks. There was an iron railing on the bow. Sierra frowned, clearly uninterested. You would think that she would have been impressed, considering that it was one of her first times seeing a boat up close, but I was wrong. She muttered, "Let's move on." I shrugged and followed her as she walked along the shore. Sierra was now far ahead of me, and even in the darkness, I could still see the shimmer in her eyes as she came across a vast boat. She motioned for me to hurry up, and I sprinted to catch up. As we neared the boat, I too had a certain gleam in my eyes.

The boat was larger than usual—a houseboat, from the looks of it. Peering through the windows, I glanced around at the modern amenities and marveled at the fact that this looked so similar to a real house. The hull of the houseboat was made of sturdy wooden planks, and the roof was made of metal shingles. The exterior was painted white. It was only one floor, but it was remarkable. A white railing stretched around the perimeter of the porch. The paint was chipped, but only a little. There were many windows that offered a pleasant view of the beach. Rows of plants bordered the patio chairs that were cushioned in striped blues and whites.

We scurried onto the dock. The boat's door was locked, of course.

Surprising me, Sierra pulled a bobby pin from her back pocket and twisted it in the lock to get the door open. "After nine years of housebreaking and pickpocketing, I know a thing or two," she confessed. Again, she surprised me.

Inside, everything was simple, beautiful, and elegant. It was like I had entered a dream. When I looked at the interior of the houseboat, I didn't just see furniture or fixtures; I saw an escape. To the right was a light gray sofa layered with soft throws. On the left was a cream vanity with gold knobs. Beyond that was a gleaming modern kitchen. The place looked like a magazine cover. I was so afraid to disturb anything, for fear that I might wrinkle the spotless sofa or leave sand all over the pristine floor.

Everything was silent except for the soft sound of the waves. It was awkward at first. We had no idea what to do. Should we head back? Stay for a while?

I startled when Sierra spoke rather loudly. I didn't know much about her, but I would have guessed she was the shy one—the girl who sat alone at the lunch table. But even the shy ones had life in them. "Angelee," she said, "haven't you ever just wanted to get away for a while? I mean, what's the point of living here, anyway? We could leave, you know. Fleur is busy, plus the watchmen are probably sleeping, and the security cameras don't pick up sound. We've been trapped here our whole lives. Don't you ever just want to see the world? There's so much out there, and there's nothing left here. We've never tried new food or seen new people or heard new languages. Life is so short, and I feel like I haven't done enough or seen enough. I want so much more than what I have. And right now, we have a chance. We have a chance!" she repeated, her face lighting up.

It took a while for me to grasp her words. Of course I had thought about leaving Calabria before—but that was just a dream, and I always woke up. Donna had even mentioned the idea to me in her bead shop, but that hope was long gone. Sierra was a Devil though. She had nothing, right? Unlike her, I had a comfortable life. What about my home, and my parents, and the vineyard? How was I supposed to leave all of those things behind? But maybe it would be easier than I thought. My parents wouldn't care anyway, and my house wasn't as meaningful anymore; it felt like a prison cell.

I didn't have time to think. The moment stretched out between us. Sierra waited patiently, though I could tell she was getting aggravated. Would I do it? I didn't exactly know. The clock was ticking; I had to make a decision quickly. Yes or no? Stay or go? In my mind, I chose Calabria, but my heart was telling me to leave this prison I was trapped in. There was no point in staying any longer. I would have more of a life out there than here. I would have more of a life *anywhere* but here.

"Let's leave" was all I said, yet it was enough to make her smile.

But now we were both questioning this decision we had made. Where would we go? What would we do? How were we supposed to make a living? What about our parents and our friends? Would we even survive? There were so many questions, and so little time to answer them. Soon we would have to head back and return to our regular lives. This was our only chance to make a change.

It was now or never.

SIERRA

I was left alone in the boat. Angelee had chosen to go back to her parents. She had gotten my hopes up when she said she wanted to leave with me, but just as quickly, my hopes came crashing down when she went in the opposite direction.

I just stayed there solo in the rays of the moon leaking through the skylights. I wasn't lonely; in fact, I preferred to be alone at that moment. I had no one to go back to. My father was still at work, the Anands would probably forget about me within a day, and Fleur would return to her dictator schedule.

But Angelee would not forget me. I had told her to meet me back here tomorrow night. Although she was planning to leave town with her family, she didn't mind delaying their travels. She said that I should bring water from the woods, and she would bring the food. Obviously, I was excited beyond belief to leave the little region of Calabria, but a part of me was so nervous that I felt sick to my stomach. How would I tell my father—or would I not even bother to say a word? And did I even trust Angelee? She seemed nice, but it was always hard to tell with Angels. And then, what if Fleur caught us? Would we both be executed?

The first step was to get off the boat. I had spent enough time contemplating when I could have been at home. I sprinted out to the dock and retraced the route that Angelee and I had followed. It felt weird to run alone in the eerie dark of the night with the stars as my only source of light. I tried to run as fast as I could, down the streets and through the village, hoping to catch up with Angelee, but it was a lost cause. The streetlamps were flickering. They were only on for a certain amount of time, because Fleur had set a curfew, restricting us from leaving our homes from 3:00 a.m. to 5:00 a.m. That meant we would only have two hours to make our escape.

I was getting closer to the street where Angelee and I had first met. I continued running and running. I was afraid of the night now, especially since I was by myself. Thankfully, I could still see the silhouettes of Fleur and the Anands up ahead.

As I approached, Fleur smiled at me warmly, while the Anands stood expressionless. Why was Fleur camouflaging her cruelty? Was it because she wanted me to trust her? Did she expect me to listen to her?

Fleur told me in a sincere voice, "Angelee will be coming with us while her parents go on a short voyage. Does that sound alright?"

I nodded reluctantly, even though I was unsure of where we were headed, and slipped into the back seat of her car. I glanced at Angelee, who waved to her parents. Mrs. Anand leaned in for a kiss on the cheek, but Angelee disregarded her and instead walked towards Fleur's car. She jumped into the back seat with me and gave a little nod for the dictator to drive off. I watched as both of the Anands sighed before fading from view.

Fleur talked gently to us, as if any loud noise would ruin the moment. "Girls, both of you will be staying at my house for three nights. You two are the first Angel and Devil paired soulmates that Calabria have ever seen. I want to make sure everything goes smoothly for the first few days. I've notified your parents. I'll prepare a snack once we arrive. You must be hungry from your long walk to Scilla beach."

Angelee was frowning, but that wasn't a surprise. She was upset that we would be staying in Fleur's mansion, not the penthouse she owned on the third floor of the municipal building. I, on the other hand, was ecstatic. I had never been inside a mansion, let alone the dictator's mansion. It would surely be an amazing experience. But Angelee seemed disoriented. I guessed there was no escaping anymore. I wanted it so badly; I wanted to leave.

"But my parents will only be on their little getaway for two days," Angelee protested. "We were going to stay for at least a week, but they can't afford to take time off from work, so they'll be home soon. So, why are we staying three nights?"

I was frustrated at Angelee. Did she really intend to ruin this opportunity for me?

Fleur shook her head disappointedly. "I'm only following your parents' instructions. I guess they just didn't want you cooped up in the house doing nothing when you could be in our company. Obviously, some days I'll have to work, but I'll be doing it remotely from home."

Angelee nodded. I could tell she was hurt from the way she immediately turned quiet.

The conversation quieted as we drove on. The region of Calabria wasn't very big, just a little under six thousand square miles. So far, it had been half an hour of silence. Fleur didn't bother to turn the radio on; there was no signal where we were. We were now in the province of Crotone, where the Devils lived—where I lived. The only signal was in the Angels' province, Cozensa. Finally, I couldn't take it anymore and started humming a random tune I had heard my dad hum.

Angelee locked eyes with me, wearing a strange expression. "That melody sounds familiar. Hum it again."

I did. Finally, she nodded. Her tone grew quiet as she spoke. "I was adopted, although you probably already knew that. And I think my biological mother used to hum that to me every night. I can hardly remember though." I nodded. Angelee continued, "I haven't seen your parents. Will I get to meet them soon?"

My heart throbbed painfully. My "parents." No, I had a "parent." I didn't want to think about it. I didn't know how people could overcome things so easily. It had been almost ten years, and I still missed my mother every day. I couldn't even get over the fact that she was dead.

Angelee waited for a response, but when she didn't get one, she hugged me comfortingly. "Is something not right?" she questioned.

I looked her dead in the eye. Of course something wasn't right! Hadn't she noticed that uncomfortable silence between us? It bothered me so much that she seemed less intelligent than me, even though she had been given more opportunities. I wanted to pierce Angelee through the heart, not with weapons, but with words. But I had to stay calm; I couldn't act indignant in front of the dictator. Who knew what she would do to me? I took deep breaths in and out, trying to keep it quiet so Fleur wouldn't sense any trouble.

The scenery had changed dramatically, from pine trees to tall willows rooted deep in the forest floor. It was warmer as well, and as the temperature rose, my nerves calmed. We were now driving up a seemingly endless road along a deep valley. Below us was a field that stretched all the way to the northern horizon. Above us were the mountains, covered with a scattering of half-melted snow and pine trees. The Botte Donato was the highest peak in the La Silla mountain range. I knew we were getting close to Fleur's mansion, because the Botte Donato mountain range was right in the middle of the province of Cosenza, where the Angels lived.

No one really knew whether the dictator was classified as a Devil or an Angel. Maybe she was neither, but that information was kept private, for only her to know. I personally believed that she was an Angel. After all, she was the one who had created the system, and she would've chosen the better of the two sides. She had practically everything she could ever wish for: the lavish home, the riches, the opportunities. Yet it seemed she did not have happiness. Every day, she woke up in the morning feeling guilty about the world she had created. In a way, Fleur was the poorest of us all. She didn't have family or love or friends—all the things that made even the poorest person wealthy.

Fleur wasn't an Angel. Fleur was a Devil.

ANGELEE

Sierra hadn't spoken to me in a while. Had I done something wrong? I honestly didn't have the strength or the courage to apologize for whatever I supposedly did. Once we arrived at the dictator's mansion, we would probably go our separate ways.

Soulmates were supposed to get along though, right? But I felt like I was the only one putting in the effort. I was the one who started all the conversations and gave all the compliments. Sierra had to try to socialize with me. I couldn't handle sitting in silence any longer, and I could tell that the dictator was thinking the same thing. I didn't say anything. Sierra didn't either. Five more minutes of silence, five more minutes of utterly confusing thoughts. And then we finally arrived at the mansion.

I gawked at the sight of Fleur's palazzo. It was clearly an even classier residence than mine, very elegant, with touches of Victorian architecture. The walls were a light salmon color, with cream-colored arches and columns, and everything fit together so perfectly. There was also an expansive front porch. On top of that, so many other accents of the house made a huge impact. Although the touches were subtle, they didn't go unnoticed: the stained glass, the sunburst panel, the bay windows, the fish scale shingles, and the stucco exterior, just to name a few.

Although the dictator didn't have her own vineyard like we did, she did have a large pool that I imagined would be refreshing on a hot summer day. Pool chairs surrounded the perimeter, cushioned with embroidered satin pillows—luxury at its finest. Adjacent to the pool was a hot tub. Both the hot tub and the pool were visible from the front of the house; Fleur obviously wanted her wealth to be appreciated. There was a mini bar opposite the pool, and as if they were meant for us, three drinks were already positioned on the white wooden counter. All three were mocktails: one a fizzy soda, one a cold juice, and one a hot tea.

As we approached the mini bar, Fleur said in a tender tone, "Those are for you over there," motioning in the direction of the drinks. "The tea is mine, but choose whichever of the other two you like. Angelee, I think you would find the fresh-squeezed juice intriguing. I hope that suits your palate. You're probably a hard one to please."

I stared down at the ground. What she said wasn't a complete lie, so I couldn't take offense to it.

She continued, "And Sierra, I know you've probably never had a drink made just for you, so I wanted to give you something unique. It's definitely a distinctive soda flavor, which can be good or bad—but that's life, isn't it?" Fleur spoke with a deeper meaning, as if she were trying to convey a secret message within her words.

Sierra simply nodded." Dictator—"

Fleur cut her off. "You may call me dictator if you wish, but I honestly prefer Fleur, or Ms. Toussaint. However, it's your choice."

Sierra nodded, still unsure. "Ms. Toussaint, I want to leave." And suddenly, there were more tears.

Fleur watched intently but didn't say anything. Perhaps she was waiting for Sierra to calm down.

"We've been trapped here in Calabria forever," Sierra sobbed. "Why?"

"Sierra…" She paused. "It's a hard subject to discuss. I knew I had to make these laws; otherwise, the world would never change or improve. This is benefitting you, and one day you'll understand. I have to be honest though: I'm thinking about doing away with the Angel and Devil classes. I'm beginning to understand that it's useless to classify people into groups based on their wealth alone. But for now, we will maintain the soulmate system. It was important for my sister, and it's just as important now, even though she's no longer with us. And as for your original question, I didn't want anyone to leave. I knew they would, if they had the opportunity. You see, people despise discipline, and they certainly do not want consequences. People ultimately wish to do whatever they please. But those people have gotten to do what they wanted to do for so long, and now it's time that they learn to control themselves and listen. I couldn't just let them off so easily. I know this is a cruel thing to do, but the people must have some sort of punishment for what they've done to this world."

Sierra nodded. At first she didn't bother to say anything, but once she'd had a chance to digest Fleur's words, she spoke. "Ms. Toussaint, I want to see the world. I don't want to be confined to this region. I'm sorry, but I finally have the courage to tell you this. Please don't punish me for telling you the truth."

The dictator nodded solemnly. "Oh, darling, I didn't mean for you to be afraid of me. I just want people to listen to me and take me seriously. I guess that's why I act in such a way. But no matter how much you'd like to leave, I can't let you. This is a small region, and word gets around quickly, and soon everyone will want to leave. I can't allow myself to look bad."

Sierra smirked. "This is for your own benefit." Sierra had a way about her; with only six words, she managed to make an impact.

"It's only you that you care about. You don't want your power taken away." How a whisper could be so forceful, I didn't know.

"I'm sorry." Fleur was beginning to cry softly. "It's hard sometimes. I often have more guilt than I do power. Sierra, if you really feel like leaving, then go for it. I can't stop you anymore. I realize that I've held people here for too long. I was young and naive back then. You must forgive me. Please don't judge me because of my past. I will change in the future."

Sierra stifled a laugh. "It's my fault as well. I shouldn't have asked to leave."

The dictator shook her head. "You cannot choose the life you are given, no matter how good or bad it may turn out to be. But you can still change your perception of the world, and even if you were born a Devil, Sierra, you're still an Angel. I've been trying to change my views on life, and as I've gotten older, I'm realizing more often that I'm not always right. In fact, I've been wrong for much of my life. I think the reason I became a dictator was because I believed that my sister was the one my parents loved more. I thought she was the favorite. I wanted to prove to my parents that I could do more than they expected of me. I had a lot of confidence in myself to make up for the lack of my parents' confidence in me. I believed it was the right decision to lead Calabria, so I created new laws, which ultimately weren't relevant or right. But again, I wanted to prove something. When my sister died, I felt like I had to do even more, be even more. So, I created the soulmate system in memory of my sister's belief in gender equality, to fulfill her ungranted wishes. But I'm realizing that I don't have to please everyone."

"Angelee wants to leave too," Sierra blurted out.

I stared at the palms of my hands, embarrassed.

Fleur smiled, but it gradually turned into a frown. "Sierra, you and only you are allowed to leave. I don't want leaving to become the next big thing," she said strictly as she peered at me. She shifted her stance, this time facing my soulmate. "And you. You are not allowed to explain to anyone about your situation. That is strictly forbidden, understand?"

I watched as an undeniable glow returned to Sierra's face, her smile fueled by the excitement of her voyage, but her strained emotion kindled by the sympathy she felt for me. "Just to be clear, am I leaving tomorrow?" she asked.

"No, not quite yet. There are still things that have to be done. Transportation, location, and above all, permission from your father. This will be a learning experience for me as well. Of course I want discipline, but I've already given too much of it. I didn't realize how much of an effect my power would have on Calabria. I still want discipline, so that I can rule, but in a more subtle way. I want discipline to play a minor role, but still contribute to the bigger picture of Calabria. Understand?"

Sierra nodded, yet I could tell she was still uncertain.

I tried to make sense of the conversation. I hadn't really accepted the fact that Sierra would be going alone, though perhaps she was being given this opportunity for a reason. Maybe she needed it more than me. After all, I was an Angel, and she was a Devil. But then again, Fleur had said the wealth classifications would be dropped. So, Sierra might have been given this opportunity because she would be more responsible with it. Or maybe it was just because she was the one who asked for it?

I had never seen Fleur be so fair, so kind and even-tempered. It was unlike her to just let things go, to permit anything illegal. There must have been something wrong.

After a short exchange, Fleur excused herself; she had some work to attend to. Sierra immediately grabbed my hand, filled with excitement that I couldn't share with her. "So," she declared, "it's crazy, isn't it?" She continued on as if she didn't expect an answer from me. I appreciated that, since I wasn't in the mood to speak to her. "I'm sorry though, Angelee. I know you would have loved to come."

The apology wasn't enough. I wanted more. I wanted to go with her.

"Maybe we can speak to her again? Maybe she'll allow you to come too. I don't even know why she's allowing me to leave. I know she said it was because she wants discipline to take a more minor role, but that still doesn't explain how she could make all these laws about no one leaving Calabria, and then just decide to let me go… But anyway, she told us to head inside. The butler will lead us to our rooms."

I just nodded, and she was fine with that.

The interior of the house was as beautiful as the outside, if not more so. There were touches of both modern and bohemian styles. The most impressive part of the house was the intricate woodwork. The color scheme of the house was much like my own. The floors were stained a dark brown, quite a bit darker than ours back home. The walls and arches were pure white. As soon as I entered the foyer, I noticed the ornate sconces placed on either side of the doorway. There was a large crystal chandelier hanging from the ceiling. The furniture was simple, yet luxurious, hued in earthy tones.

A butler stood in the foyer. His face was expressionless as he guided us through a long hallway towards our temporary bedrooms. On the walls were all kinds of mirrors in no particular pattern. They all had the same vibrant gold trim, and there was not a single fingerprint to be seen on any of them. I was sure Fleur had told her servants to handle them with care. It didn't even occur to me that the dictator only employed male servants, chauffeurs, and butlers; I guess my mind was elsewhere.

It seemed like it came as a shock when Sierra realized she had her own room, as she had most likely imagined us sharing a bedroom. The butler led us to my room first. He offered me a choice of several amenities, including a rose-scented bar of soap and little bottles of shampoo and conditioner.

I stepped into my room and slammed the door behind me. I didn't mean to be aggressive, but I just felt like letting everything out. I just wanted time—time to process everything that had happened over the last few days. My bottled-up thoughts and emotions couldn't just sit silently within me anymore. I didn't bother to lock the bedroom door; I didn't care if someone walked in on me weeping. I felt more alone than I had in a long time. There was no way to describe the sensation I was feeling. It was even worse than sadness.

Though I was upset, I still appreciated the beauty of the room. It was plain and simple, light and airy. It smelled like citrus. There was even a platter with a flaky, buttery croissant on the nightstand. There was only a twin bed in the room, pushed against a window that framed the trees outside. Beyond that was an aged door, which probably led to the bathroom. Curious as to what the bathroom looked like, I wiped away the tears that clung to my cheeks and gently pulled open the door.

The bathroom, just like the bedroom, was breathtaking. The minimalistic design created an even bolder impression. On the counter was a glass containing an orange liquid. I decided to try it. Contrary to my expectations, it tasted even sweeter than an orange and more tart. But then I realized it wasn't orange juice; it was actually mango lassi. The yogurt-based texture was thicker than orange juice, and it brought back so many sweet memories from my childhood. During the summer, my mother would make me a mango lassi every single day once she was finished with work. She would make one for herself as well, and we would sit in the vineyard, sipping our lassi on one of the wooden benches. It was crazy how so many things had changed so quickly.

I gripped the mango lassi in my hands, afraid that if I let go, I would lose all the memories that came along with it. There was another time, the first time I had ever tasted it, when I had been sitting silently with my Nani on a checkered picnic blanket in her backyard. My mood had been sullen, though I had forgotten the reason why. Neither of us made a peep, counting on the gentle wind to do the talking for us. There was a picnic basket beside my grandmother's bare feet. Noticing my mood, she pulled out a pitcher of the mango yogurt drink, poured some into a small glass cup, and handed it to me. She urged me to take a small sip, and I reluctantly agreed. It was the sweetest thing I had ever tasted.

She knew I was sad and scared. She knew silence wouldn't heal me, and so she helped. It was painful to think about her, now that she was gone. The scariest part for me was the fear of losing the memories and moments I had shared with her. In the wake of her passing, I felt as if at any moment, everything I knew about her would evaporate into thin air, and I would be left with nothing.

Abruptly, I smashed the glass down on the counter. I couldn't help it; everything felt as if it were moving in slow motion. A million little pieces of glass burst into the air. The bright liquid flew everywhere and I couldn't help but notice how sweet it smelled. The shards rained down musically on the counter and floor, the delicious drink collapsed at my feet in a little rippling pool. And then everything came back up to speed again.

A fragment of glass stabbed one of my toes. As I lifted my feet from the wooden tiles of the Victorian bathroom, I glanced at myself in the mirror. My cheeks were hollow, my body skinny, my teeth yellow, my hair disheveled. I looked more like myself again, yet I still felt like a stranger in my own body. Where had the Angel in me gone?

I wondered how Sierra was doing. Without a doubt, she was much better than me. She was alright, I was sure. She was kind and quite intelligent, considering the minimal education she had received. She was friendly, and I couldn't help but compare myself to her. She had nothing, and yet she was everything. I had everything, and yet I was nothing.

SIERRA

The butler led me to my room, taking slow steps in his polished leather shoes. He gave me an eerily soothing smile as I arrived.

I gracefully shut the door to my room. The first thing I observed was the ceiling, painted a light blue with drifting clouds. Enchanting, but I didn't care much about the room. It was a luxury in itself to be lodging here, and that was truly the only thing I cared about. I had my own bathroom, which was lovely. The twin-sized bed was much more comfortable than the one at home. Noting that the nightstand only had two drawers, I realized I had nothing to store—no toiletries or clothes.

From the corner of my eye, I noticed a Charlotte cake atop the nightstand. My mother used to serve it to me. She would bake it fresh for my birthday. On those special days when she would receive a large cash bonus, she would purchase the ingredients that were used to make the dessert. It was typically served hot, but my mother knew I preferred it cold. She would line a mold with sponge cake and then add a layer of strawberry puree. It was my favorite thing in the entire world. Fleur must have somehow known this; why else would she have placed it in a crystal cake dome? Perhaps she didn't want me to leave. She wanted me to cling to my memories of home, my memories of my mother. She knew that if I left Calabria, I would be leaving those behind. She wanted to remind me of my past. She wanted me to realize that I had to stay with the remains of my mother and what little was left of my father. It was as if she had overheard that conversation between Angelee and me at the fishing port, saying we wanted to leave. Now she was encouraging us not to.

But it still didn't quite make sense. Why had she told me I could leave? Was it because she wanted us to think she was on our side? Or was it because she respected our views and dreams? But then, why would she also want us to stay? Did she want us to do both, Angelee staying here and going on with her life, but me leaving?

Fleur would never just let me go because I desired to, or because I requested it. It was probably because she wanted me to do something for her, complete some kind of task. But then again, why would she choose me to complete that task? Why not Angelee? Was it because I was a Devil, and she was an Angel? Perhaps only a Devil could complete the type of task she would send me off to do.

I could barely think straight. My mind was a mess, as well as my appearance. I needed sleep. I crawled into the bed and pulled the covers over my head, and that was all I remembered.

I awoke to a gentle knock on my door, but I didn't feel up to getting up to answer it. I couldn't even talk; my throat felt scratchy and sore. The door opened anyway, and it was Fleur, of course. Who else was I expecting? Angelee?

Fleur sighed, and I knew we were both thinking the same thing. I had slept too long. She pulled open the silk curtains, and the sky outside was an inky blue, sparkling with stars. She stood beside the bed and spoke to me in a quiet voice, so as to not wake me up fully. "Sierra, your Charlotte cake was good?"

I nodded, though I had not even tasted it. She was pulling me closer to home—but the more I thought about home, the more I wanted to leave Calabria.

"Darling, we have to discuss your voyage." I sat up, more awake. "First things first: where would you even travel to?" She answered the question on her own, as if she had already taken the time to think about it. "I was thinking about France. The small town of Blesle, to be precise."

"Isn't that where you grew up?" I asked.

She continued without answering, "I feel like I can be honest with you. There have been several sightings of my sister in that town. People are telling me she's still alive."

I blinked, taken aback. "Well, do you believe it?"

"I don't exactly know. But besides that, you want to leave, and I want to find my sister, if she's still alive. So, it works for both of us."

"Why can't you just go yourself? I don't understand why you're sending me."

"One question at a time." Fleur laughed, but she could tell I was not that easily amused. She continued, "It's just not that easy. I have a job. I'm a leader. I have to be loyal, and if others aren't allowed to leave Calabria, then neither am I. I enforced all these rules on the citizens to initiate change in the world, but I never applied those same rules to myself. And if one person isn't following those measures, then the world will never change. And the reason I want to send you is not just because you want to leave. It's because you think you're afraid."

I had no idea what in the world she was saying. Thankfully, she completed her thought. "You think you're afraid of jumping from a great height, of change and exploring new things. You think you're afraid because you've never seen the world. You don't know what's out there. But being afraid doesn't mean you back away from things, or that you don't have the strength to commit. No, being afraid means nothing. But you'll never learn that if you don't see the world for yourself. You have to know that being afraid isn't bad. You can't pretend anymore that the things you're afraid of aren't there; you have to face them. And the only way to do that is to go see the world. Don't be afraid of something that will set you free. Don't be fearful, dear. This is the moment you've been waiting for your entire life."

I felt excitement mixed with fear. "I can't imagine that, because I've been trapped here for so long. It's so much easier to say than do. This isn't just a dream; this is reality for me."

"I know, Sierra. I can't apologize anymore though. People tell me that I'm evil, but I have to gain confidence in myself. In a way, it's similar to what I just taught you."

All I could do was smile slightly; I didn't have the energy to do much more. She left the room before I could say anything else.

A knock on the door startled me. I had just fallen back to sleep, and this was the last thing I needed. But when I opened the door, no one was there, just a small letter with no envelope, written in a barely legible scrawl. It seemed to be a list of some kind. I read the letter to myself out loud, it was a habit.

"'Dear Ms. Sierra, I am happy to inform you that you will be leaving for the small French town of Blesle on August 31, 2347. As you may know, there have been sightings of my sister, Chantelle. You will be dropped off at the airport by me personally, and I will arrange for someone to escort you around Blesle and answer any questions you may have. You will be leaving from the Reggio Calabria airport. The airport hasn't been used in a long time, due to traveling restrictions. However, I am making an exception, as I will be there to escort you. You are allowed to bring only one luggage item. Food, water, and other necessities will be provided along the way. We have called your father to inform him of the voyage you will be taking, and he has agreed to it.'"

I stopped reading. Well, of course he had agreed to it! He had no choice. I continued reading aloud.

"'You will be allowed to see your father for the duration of one day before you leave for France on August 31. Angelee will be staying with me as well until September 1, because her parents will be away for longer than expected. If you have any questions, please feel free to ask me anything. Make sure to pack your bag immediately, as you only have a few days to prepare. Thank you for your cooperation during this time. Sincerely, Fleur Toussaint, dictator of Calabria.'"

As I finished reading the letter, my mind was spinning. It was a lot to think about. I assumed that within two days, I would be spending the day with my father. Tomorrow, I would spend all day packing and have some time to catch up with Angelee.

There was an awful pain in my stomach: hunger. The past few years, I had felt as if I were immune to feeling hungry, like I had outgrown it. But for some reason, I really felt like putting something in my stomach. I didn't even take into account the Charlotte cake still sitting on my nightstand, instead slipping quietly down the hallway towards Angelee's room.

ANGELEE

I heard a slow creak, signaling that someone had just entered my room. I shut the bathroom door, making sure no one would find me crying on the floor, especially Fleur. But when I heard Sierra's voice, I felt a sensation of relief wash over me.

"Angelee, would you please let me in?" I reluctantly agreed. Her words spilled out in a rush. "Fleur wrote me a letter. It's long, so I'll be brief. On August thirty-first, I'm leaving for the town of Blesle, where Fleur grew up!"

I didn't bother to ask any questions; I knew she would answer them on her own. That was one of the great things about Sierra: she seemed to know what you were thinking even before you did.

"I'm going there because several people in the village claim to have seen Fleur's sister, Chantelle, in Blesle," she continued. "And my father knows about this too; I believe Fleur gave him a call. Obviously, he can't be pleased that I'm going, but what can he do? But on a positive note, I'll get to see him a couple days before I leave."

Another thing I valued about Sierra was that she always managed to find a way to be positive in any situation. I really wished I could be more like her, more content and delighted by the little things.

She continued, and I was glad that she took the time to explain my end of the situation. "Fleur has extended your stay here until

September first. Your parents are extending their excursion." She looked concerned. "I don't know when I'm coming back. Fleur partly believes that her sister is still alive, but maybe that's just wishful thinking. She probably doesn't want me to come back before I find her though, so it may take a while."

Was I supposed to say something, give her some sort of reaction? I was empty; I had nothing to say. I managed to choke a few words out though. All I could say was, "I'll miss you." But I could have said, *"I'm here for you if you need anything,"* or *"Don't forget about me,"* or even *"You deserve this. Even if it takes time to find Chantelle, you've earned this more than anyone."* But instead, I only managed to say the lamest thing that could come out of my mouth.

Sierra smiled. I could tell it wasn't a fake smile; she meant it. "I won't," she said boldly, and that made it hurt even more. I was so close to leaving the room, but when she spoke, I listened. "I didn't mean it like that, just that I hoped that you would come with me. You could, you know—at least, if you want to."

I stopped, taking some time to decide how to reply. I would have loved to go with her, but there were more consequences than opportunities. "We could never pull that off," I murmured.

"Sure we could! It would be fun! Fleur explained in her letter that I'll have a personal escort. You could disguise yourself as one." But I could tell by her exaggerated chuckle that she meant none of it. I guessed she didn't really want me to go with her. Or maybe it was just in my head; I had so much self-doubt and insecurity that I thought no one liked me. But what if she really did? What if all those thoughts were just in my head? What if that chuckle meant friendship? It was always hard to tell with people like Sierra. She was so nice that sometimes you assumed it was an act, and she was just following the words off of her script.

Sierra waited several moments before saying anything else. "Angelee, are you okay?" I guessed she could see in my eyes that I was not okay—far from it. "You can tell me, you know."

I nodded. "I wish I could be more like you," I said, biting my lip in pure embarrassment. She nodded thoughtfully, but didn't say anything in return, so I continued, "You've been through so much more than me, but even still, you manage to keep that smile on your face. How are you so perfect all the time?"

She shook her head. "Don't wish to be me. I'm just hiding everything—all my emotions and pain. I don't want anyone to see my weakness. You're doing what's right; you aren't afraid to cry or yell. I am though."

I smiled sympathetically. "I just want you to know that you're probably the only person who will ever leave Calabria, and I'm so happy for you. I want you to go on your own and experience things that I never will. But at the same time, I want to go with you. I want to see the world. I want to *feel* the world. I want to live free, because we don't get that chance here. I really want to go. And I understand if you want to do those things for yourself, if you want the credit of being the first person to leave these borders. But I need to escape, just for a little while."

I must have made it hard to say no, because next thing I knew, we were sneaking down to the kitchen and excitedly discussing our plans for a short escape to Blesle together.

SIERRA

Dinner wasn't much of a meal, but it was much better than what I was used to. We had snuck into one of Fleur's kitchens. There were three. The first was for her use, the second was for the servants, and the third was inexplicably left untouched. We snuck into the second one, because we knew the third had no food, and if we were caught in the servants' kitchen, we would get into significantly less trouble.

No one was in the kitchen. Everyone must have fallen asleep long before. There were no lights on, and we couldn't manage to find the light switch. In the darkness, Angelee and I clung to each other nervously. Thankfully, the windows opposite the fridge let in enough moonlight for us to at least see each other's silhouettes. Even in the dark, we could see that the kitchen was kept tidy, exactly how the dictator liked it. Everything was in its place.

It was Angelee who decided to risk looking in the fridge. There was leftover stew, as well as chicken legs, but she was a vegetarian. I didn't have that luxury; I had to hunt to survive. She brought out a big bowl of salad, which she split into two servings for us.

When we finished, I was still hungry. I loved dessert, but it was such a rare treat for me. Now I finally had the opportunity, so I scoured every cabinet in hopes of finding something sweet. To me, dessert was a big deal, a luxury my father and I could never afford. So, I was disappointed when I couldn't find anything. The lettuce and cherry tomatoes would have to be enough for now. We retreated back to our separate rooms, leaving the kitchen just the way it was.

I lay in bed, thinking. The curtains were closed, and the steady hum of rain against the roof was the only sound. Sleeping was challenging for me, even on a normal day—and it seemed like it hadn't been normal for a long, long time. The cozy blanket beckoned me to shut my eyes, the bed swallowing me whole, but I still found it difficult to doze off.

An hour passed, and then another. My eyes were still open. I wasn't even thinking or dreaming anymore. Everything was cleared out of my mind—the past, the present, the future. And I wanted it to stay that way.

Sometimes all you had to do was not think. You could just let everything happen without worry or doubt. You began to see the world differently, as if the fog had finally been cleared off the lens. For that one moment, everything seemed to fall into place, and everything felt at peace. The world was much simpler. Every question had an answer, and there was no need for cruelty or jealousy or sadness.

I had been only eight years old when my mother died. My whole world had stopped. My dad didn't come out of his room for days at a time, and I had no one but myself. In the days after she died, she was all I could think about. My father seemed to cry every day. Two months after my mother's death, he was still holed up in his room. He never turned on a light or opened the blinds. I wasn't sure what he did in there, but I assumed he was contemplating his life decisions.

It was three months after my mother passed when I had stopped to think about my own choices. I remembered something that a farmer told me around that time. I used to travel to the fields, because I had nothing else with which to occupy myself, and I would stand at the gate that separated the houses from the plots of land, curiously watching the men as they completed their labor. There was one farmer who worked in the farthest field. Even though he worked all the way in the back, that didn't stop him from making his way over to me every day and bringing me a bunch of raspberries. I could still taste them in my mouth, sweet like summer. I wished I knew his name; I would have loved to repay him.

One day, he came over and gave me his usual raspberries. He had heard about my mother's death, and the hardships my father and I were facing. He gave me the best advice I had ever received. "You will never get over it; you'll always miss her," he said solemnly. "Its's the sad and bitter truth—but you will change because of this loss. You'll become stronger because of it. You aren't alone, you know. I've been through it too, just like almost everybody else. So, listen to me, you're breaking your own heart right now by crying and grieving. What does your mother want for you?" he asked sincerely.

Being my young and innocent self, I said, "I'm not sure."

"I promise you, she just wants you to be happy. She wouldn't want you crying every single day. It's normal to feel sad, and it's important to let yourself feel these emotions, but not forever. Like I said, you're just breaking your own heart by thinking about her. I promise that she'll always be there, looking down on you, knowing that you're okay. It's a burden for her as well, knowing you're sad. So, try to keep a smile on your face, kid. Alright?"

"I'll try," I said wearily, and he smiled back.

The farmer had been right: I was breaking my heart thinking about her every second of every day. It was too much. I finally took the farmer's advice into account. And even though I felt bad for dismissing her from my thoughts, eventually it worked. I felt less sad, and the yearning for her presence gradually decreased.

My mind came back to reality, yet I still couldn't stop thinking of my mother. Even though she was way up in Heaven, part of her was down here with me. I guessed that's what the farmer meant: I was breaking my heart by thinking about her too much. But I could still feel her with me. She was in the trees of the woods. She was beneath the surface of the lake we used to swim in. She was in our cramped apartment, brushing her thick hair while sitting on the kitchen floor. She was found in me too, in my heart and mind. She was there in the Charlotte cake she'd once made me. She was rooted in my personality, my hopes, my dreams.

An hour later, I was dead to the world. Sleep had finally overcome me, and I definitely wouldn't be waking up until at least noon.

ANGELEE

I wasn't hungry at all. The butlers were trying to force me to eat, but I declined.

I patiently waited for Sierra to wake up. I didn't feel like waking her; she deserved rest, and she needed it too. I wandered down the hallway, pacing back and forth. No one was really awake yet, besides me and few of the many servants. Fleur must've still been sleeping too. So, I sat in the sunlight flooding in through the large windows and waited for Sierra to crawl out of bed. I occupied myself by twisting strands of my tangled hair around my finger and shutting my eyes, letting the whole world close in on me.

It must have been an hour before Sierra met up with me in the hallway. She tapped me gently on the shoulder, then accompanied me to the dining hall. Fleur was already at the table, seated by a young girl I didn't recognize. She looked a couple years older than me, perhaps in her last year of school. The girl stood up to greet us and shake our hands. She had a firm grip, along with large, friendly brown eyes, and her hair was almost black. Her clothes were tight-fitting, and her shirt barely came past her belly button.

I sat adjacent to Fleur. Sierra was opposite her, so they could easily converse, while the young lady was facing me. The other seats stood empty. Large amounts of delicious food covered the table. I reached for a roll, smothering it in apricot jam, even though my stomach could barely hold it.

After a long period of awkward silence, Fleur started the conversation in an uneasy tone. "Sierra, this is Jia. She was sent here from the province of Hubei in central China. She will be your chaperone for your trip to Blesle. Jia won a raffle at her school and was selected to come here. It's a prestigious award, one that she won't waste. I sent for her early, so you could have time to meet. After all, you'll be spending quite a lot of time with her, and we wouldn't want you two to not get along, now would we?"

Sierra and Jia both shook their heads. I could tell that Jia was just as bewildered as Sierra.

The meal resumed just as awkwardly. Fleur was the only one talking, while the rest of us just nodded or shook our heads in response. I could tell that the dictator was alright with that; she preferred the spotlight on herself.

After I had stuffed myself far too much, Sierra and Jia went off to play some sort of icebreaker game, and I was left alone once again. Fleur told me I could feel free to explore her house. She would be in her office, preparing for Sierra's voyage to France. Through all the chaos—the butlers scurrying, the servants dusting, the chefs baking—I could still make out the hope in the dictator's eyes. It was obvious that more than anything, Fleur just wanted her sister back. I couldn't blame her; her sister must have meant the world to her. After all, she had created the whole soulmate system in memory of Chantelle.

I wandered down random corridors and carpeted hallways, hoping to come across something eye-catching. I didn't even know what I was looking for—something to occupy my time? I pushed open a heavy set of French doors that led into a strange room that was quite small. All four walls were deeply curved, with a domed ceiling. A reading chair sat against one of the walls, adjacent to a small table. There was a single mirror that stood on the table, angled so that I couldn't see my reflection. I could tell no one had been in this room in a long time, as a layer of dust stretched across the surface of the mirror.

I had once heard about a room like this. They were quite rare, only to be found in certain secretive places. Their purpose was to help you talk to the dead.

I had no one to communicate with. Maybe Darlene, but I didn't really know if she was dead. I didn't want to speak with my grandmother; it would bring back terrible memories I couldn't bear to relive. Secretly, I had been longing to speak with my biological mother and father. I thought they must have been long gone by now, as they were considered unfortunate, and if they couldn't even take care of me, how could they have managed to fend for themselves?

I assumed I should speak from the heart, and I did. I spoke quietly at first, still unsure whether what I was doing was correct, then louder, with much more confidence.

"Mother, I know that I was adopted. When I first found out, I couldn't even bear the pain. The part that hurt the most was that the 'mother' I was living with isn't even related to me. But we still share the same memories, and she's always been there for me, so I hope you don't mind if I call her mother too. I know it was best for you to give me away, but sometimes I still wonder what it would be like if you hadn't. I have so much to say. I don't miss you that much though; I barely even knew you. I wish I had known you better."

I considered what else I should share. "I'm sixteen now, and I just got assigned a soulmate! Her name is Sierra, and she's leaving in a couple days for Blesle, France. But you probably already know all of this, if you're watching me from up above." My throat seared with a burning sensation. "I love you with all my heart. Please just talk to me. I want you to be here right now. Please."

I sat very still, anticipating my mother's voice, waiting for her to respond. Nothing came, but even still, I didn't dare make a noise.

After a few minutes, I silently left the room, disheartened, the weight of my mother's absence dragging me down. I jogged towards the pool, trying to find something to distract myself. The water looked calm and clear, welcoming me into its depths. Climbing onto the diving board, I lifted my legs and jumped, clothes and all. My whole body plunged feet first into the icy liquid. When I emerged, I wiped my hands over my eyes before I opened them. I dipped my hair into the pool, allowing it to completely submerge, along with all of my heavy thoughts.

SIERRA

Jia led me to a small room, located in the east wing of Fleur's mansion. The floor was white tile, and the walls were white too. Jia held what looked like a pack of flash cards in her left hand. Written on the cards were the icebreaker questions that we were supposed to answer.

Jia began first. "'What's your full name? First, middle, and last.'"

"Sierra Berlusconi. I don't have a middle name."

"Cool. You can just call me Jia."

I guess I was nervous about how she would react if I asked her her middle and last name, so I didn't say anything and let her carry on with the next question.

"'What do you want to become?'"

"Hmm, not too specific. So, I'll answer the question as *who* I want to become, not what."

"That's fair, you can continue."

I smirked. Did she really think I needed her approval? "I want to be a happy person," I said with no doubt.

She nodded and moved the card to the back of the deck. "Maybe you should ask me a question now," she said. "The dictator already told me all about you, but you know nothing about me."

She handed me the flashcards, and I shuffled the deck, looking for the right question to ask.

"'When you pass away, what do you want to be remembered for?'" I questioned.

"I don't really know yet. My parents would like me to become a violinist," Jia replied.

"No, what do *you* want to be remembered for? Not what your parents want for you."

"I'm still trying to figure that out. And you?"

"My music," I said.

"Oh, you play an instrument too?"

"I sing."

"Then let me hear something," she responded with a grin.

I didn't think much about it, just took a deep breath and began, drawing all the emotion stuck within me into a hauntingly beautiful melody.

When it was her turn to ask me a question, she seemed amazed, as if she knew there was a part of me that was as beautiful as the song I had just sung. "'Are you more of a sunrise, daytime, twilight, or nighttime kind of person?'"

"That one's easy," I said. "It's definitely sunrise for me. When my mother was still healthy, we would go to the woods. It was at that time, in the early morning, when I truly felt at peace. Together, we would watch the sun rise and the animals awaken. It was my favorite time."

"Your mother sounds like a wonderful person."

"She was." A sudden emptiness filled the room, and Jia tried to fill the space with the next question.

"'If you could live anywhere, what place would you choose and why?'"

"I … I don't know." The bitter truth stabbed me like a knife. I had only ever seen the tiny region of Calabria. Everything else seemed a world away. "Tell me, what's China like?"

"Well, where I live, there's hundreds of buildings. You can hardly see the stars at night, but the fluorescent billboard lights make up for it. The city comes alive at night. There's not that much greenery, mostly concrete and asphalt. I hadn't seen an ocean in ages until I came here."

"I don't think China is right for me," I admitted.

"It's alright. Anywhere else?" she asked.

"Greece? I've never seen it, but it's quite close to here. I'm sure it's beautiful."

"I've never been, but I've seen pictures of it online," she said.

"I've seen some pictures in magazines. We don't have access to the internet here," I explained.

"It must be hard living without the internet."

"Not really. I can't miss it if I've never had it," I responded.

"Okay, next question: 'What is the earliest childhood memory you remember?'"

"Hmm… I must have been three or four years old. My mother and my father were dancing to jazz music on the stereo. I was giggling as I watched them, and then we were all dancing together. Of course, it isn't the first thing I can remember, but it's the happiest thing I can remember," I told her.

For the next hour, we shared back and forth about our lives at home, our family, and our friends. Even though there were so many contrasting things about our lives, we also shared many similarities. It comforted me to know that there was a girl out there who had felt pain before too. We all had. That was enough.

ANGELEE

Sierra and Jia had been gone for hours. In a way, it made me feel envious. I had known Sierra longer than Jia had, yet I knew she would never spend hours on end with me like that. At first, I wanted to disrupt their friendship, but then I remembered how little happiness Sierra had enjoyed in her life. Maybe I would wait until lunchtime.

I stayed in the pool, the sun darkening my skin to a golden brown. I stretched my hand out into the depths of the numbing water. After a long while, I got out and dried myself off with one of the thick cotton towels Ms. Toussaint had set aside for me on the sun chairs in case I wanted to take a shower. I peeled off my soaking clothes and exchanged them for fresh ones that the dictator had also provided for me. Once my hair was tied back in a high bun, I started down the hallway to find Sierra and Jia. My first thought was to check the east wing, because I remembered Jia leading Sierra in that direction. Plus, it was close to the dining hall where we had eaten breakfast. But then I went with my second instinct, which was to just go to the dining room and wait for lunch to be served.

By the time I reached it, Fleur, Jia, and Sierra were already seated. I joined them quietly, as they were already midway through their conversation. Not wanting to interrupt, I grabbed a slice of buttered bread. It wasn't a surprise when I heard the other three discussing their plans for Blesle. It was a huge trip, monumental.

No one had traveled outside of Calabria for more than a decade.

The chef set a panini in front of me, per my request. Sierra and Jia were both served green tea and a pita wrap. Fleur just drank her water. Jia and Sierra were giggling the whole time, paying little to no attention to me. We weren't in middle school; they didn't have to exclude me so immaturely. Fleur occasionally joined in on the conversation, but kept to herself most of the time. I knew she was thinking about her sister, hoping that she was still alive. In the back of her mind, she must have known the chances were slim.

SIERRA

Angelee seemed more invested in her panini than in the conversation. Unlike her… I thought? I had really only known her for a couple days. So, instead of worrying about Angelee, I focused my attention on Jia. She wasn't all bad. In the beginning, I had suspected she would be much worse. But her personality was just as soft as her eyes. We turned out to be very much alike. We both came from poor families, but we had found different ways to cope with that anxiety. For her, it was the violin, and for me, it was nature. Jia was funny too. While it felt so unnatural to laugh, it felt even more unnatural to *share* a laugh. I couldn't complain; laughter felt so good.

And then my laughter stopped just as quickly as it had started. When I saw the expression on Angelee's face, it dawned on me why she was acting so weird. She stared down at her plate, her eyes tired and sad. I knew she wasn't responding this way because of Jia and me; it was because she felt unwanted, worthless, like she always had.

Angelee stiffly stood up from her chair and pushed it in softly. She excused herself from the table with only two words: "I'm done." Then she exited the room. As soon as she left, Fleur took a long sip of water. Jia glanced at me with uncertainty, but I didn't respond. Instead, I stood up and left the room too.

I found Angelee in her room. She was stretched out across the bed, staring at the ceiling. Without asking, I situated myself next to her. There was a lot of silence, which went on for too long, triggering Angelee to speak.

"Sorry," she mumbled softly.

"For what?"

"For trying to take away your happiness."

"What do you mean?" I asked.

"When I realized how long you'd spent with Jia, it made me jealous, knowing that you would rather spend time with her—"

"I had no choice," I said, distinctly irritated.

"I was just being dumb, overthinking as always. But it made me feel—"

"Unworthy? Useless?"

"Yes. Exactly."

"I get it," I said. "But when I saw you in the dining room, just staring at your plate, I couldn't help but wonder why you were sad."

She sighed. "I thought I explained this already."

"How are you even allowed to feel sad?" I demanded. "You have everything—*everything*! And then I'm happy for a single second, and you won't let me have it. You won't even let me *feel* it."

"That isn't true, and you know it," she snapped.

"Try living my life. Try having nothing. Only then are you allowed to be sad," I cried.

"Look, I know I'm lucky, and I know it seems like I have the world in the palms of my hands, but I have a right to my feelings. I have the right to feel sad when I want to. If I can't take your happiness away, then don't try to take my sadness away."

"You don't get it!" I insisted. "You've been handed so many opportunities that I haven't—an education, proper food, a nice house… Do you know how hard my dad and I had to work just for me to get a few years at school? You *do* have everything, and you know it. You can't possibly be sad, living a life like that."

Angelee remained quiet, looking even more hurt than she had at lunch. But the worst part was that I didn't feel like I had to apologize; I was so caught up in the fact that I was right. After a while, all I could do was leave the room. Angelee was still silent and didn't even bother to look at me as I left, but how could I blame her? She was an Angel.

ANGELEE

Maybe Sierra was right. What was I even thinking? Of course she was right. I guessed I had never really known how harsh life was for Devils, because I had never befriended them, never really asked them if they needed help. But that was only because I had been too blinded by my family's opulence. And suddenly, I felt as if I were slowly maturing into my parents, becoming a younger version of them.

I could hear whispers coming from outside my room. It was probably Sierra and Jia. I didn't want to enter the conversation while Jia was in it, but I still wanted to hear. I pressed my ear up against my door, waiting, though I didn't know exactly what I was waiting for.

I finally heard Jia leave Sierra's room. I waited one moment longer to avoid seeing Jia in the hallway, then met Sierra in her room.

"I'm sorry. Again," I said to her, embarrassed.

"Wow, two apologies in one day. You're on a roll," she replied sarcastically.

"I mean it though. I was acting like my parents, too blind to see what life is like for the Devils."

"It's fine. You're an Angel; how would you know?" Sierra shrugged.

"I could have spoken to Devils. I could have donated to them, or made food… I could have done so much."

"You didn't know," she repeated.

"Well, the worst part is, what if I *had* known? I feel like I wouldn't have helped either way."

"You must care though, because you keep talking about it," Sierra responded.

"Caring isn't worth anything if you don't do something about it. I've heard stories of Devils starving to death. And I cried for them—but I didn't do anything about it. If I had provided them with some food, they might be alive right now."

"I get it. I watched my mother die before my eyes, but if I had worked harder, maybe we could have gotten the money to pay for her surgeries and treatments."

"That's different. I had the resources, and you didn't." And then I wondered, would anyone save me if I were dying? Regardless of whether they had the resources or not, would anyone pull me from the jaws of death? Or would they just watch silently as I slipped away?

SIERRA

Finally, morning came. Faint scents of breakfast wafted towards me, luring me into the dining room. A large array of pastries, eggs, cereals, and juices were laid out on the table. I lunged for an apple cider waffle and some eggs Benedict, pocketing a fruit cup for later.

I was the only one sitting at the breakfast table. Jia was getting ready, Angelee was still sleeping, and Fleur was probably tapping her fingers on the steering wheel of her Bugatti Veyron. I grabbed some more fruit and ran outside. As I reached the car, I could make out four figures inside, one sitting in the driver's seat and three in the back seat. The driver was most definitely Fleur; I could see the silhouette of her feathered hat. But I couldn't quite figure out who was sitting in the back seat because of the tinted windows. I climbed into the passenger seat and realized it was Angelee sitting in the back between two bodyguards.

I already knew what the bodyguards were doing here. They were willing to protect Fleur not because people were dying for her autograph, but because it was considered honorable to work under someone powerful.

Fleur greeted me as I fastened my seat belt. "Before I drop you off at your house, we're meeting a specialist named Aryan. He will provide the proper remedy to get Angelee back to normal. Is that alright?"

I could tell she was trying her very best to seem kind. I would have liked to just nod, but curiosity overcame me. "I thought Angelee already received her required dosage."

"She received her first dose a few days ago, but she needs a second one."

"Oh, that makes more sense now."

"Happy to help," Fleur murmured earnestly, although I could tell her mind was somewhere far away.

The ride wasn't a long one; Aryan was only five miles away. Everything was silent. I felt sorry for Angelee, who was hunched between the two men. Yet it was quite humorous to see a girl as proper as her with her dress wrinkled and hair frizzed.

Everything happened faster than expected. Aryan seemed like a nice guy. Angelee drank the remedy from a mason jar. Fleur conversed with him for a span of five minutes. We all said our goodbyes, and then we got back in the car. We were headed to the province of Crotone, where I lived. Father would most likely be waiting on the porch of our apartment. He would enfold me in a warm hug and offer me a small bite of cannoli, which cost him a week's earnings. He was always kind like that, giving me all the little things in life that made the biggest impact. I loved him for that.

ANGELEE

I surveyed myself in the rearview mirror of the car. My hair was now back to normal, dark like the night. I kind of missed Fleur's blonde hair. But what I really missed was Fleur's personality. I wanted her confidence, her boldness. I needed it. I was always the girl reading a book in the corner, or crying in the middle of a party. I was the girl who only entered a conversation if I didn't have a choice. I was the girl who got frightened over little things, but tried to keep her cool in the middle of a storm.

And I wasn't polite either—not for an Angel, at least. My family and friends would have described me as half-hearted. Even Sierra seemed to be more polite than me. What I didn't get was how she could be so free when her life was so confined. I didn't understand how she could be so hopeful when nothing had gone her way, how she could be so forgiving when she'd been deprived of countless opportunities. I was none of those things. How could she be so perfect when her life was the complete opposite of perfect? And I knew she would never think these things about me. She would never dream of being me, or wish she had a quality I possessed. I was such a failure, where she was such an angel.

We were getting closer to the province of Crotone, where the Devils lived, and I was actually quite interested to see what Sierra's apartment looked like. Perhaps seeing it would ignite a spark in me. It would help me see what the Devils' lives were really like, how their lives differed from mine. I imagined that the apartment complex would be impoverished. I pictured the grass as a charred yellow, the paint cracked and worn, the windows splashed with dirt, the sidewalk uneven. And I couldn't even imagine what the interior of their apartment would be like. Scattered furniture and broken tiles? I had never set foot inside the borders of the province of Crotone. It wasn't because I had never gotten the chance, but mostly because my parents wanted me to know my worth. Their definition of perfect would mean never associating with Devils. No, life revolved around the Angels, and only the Angels.

We walked down an old cobblestone street lined with white streetlamps and perfectly manicured bushes. I was in awe of the beauty of the province. Perhaps the Devils tended to it so well because it was the only thing they had. Our province, Cozensa, was disorderly compared to theirs, because it wasn't the only thing we had or cared about.

When we arrived at the apartment, Sierra breathed a sigh of relief, and I could tell she was happy to be home. She skipped up the spiral staircase that led to the fourth floor where she lived and motioned for us to follow. Her father was already standing outside the door, arms open wide. Sierra jumped into his embrace, which made me wish even more that I had that kind of relationship with my father.

Sierra's father, Cain, greeted Fleur and me with a hug, just as he had given Sierra. "Come on in. I know it's not much, but it's our home," he said in a warm voice as he motioned me inside. "Have a seat."

We all took a seat without a word. Cain asked, "Care for any refreshments?"

Fleur, realizing she had to be the one to speak, cleared her throat. "Just water, please, no ice."

When he came back, Fleur was clearly embarrassed, as the glass was filled only a quarter of the way, and she didn't know how to react to this.

"I apologize," said Cain. "I mean, I know our leader deserves better than this, but we just don't have the water supply right now."

Fleur straightened her posture, trying to conceal her embarrassment. After all, she was the one who had caused the shortage of clean water, because most of it was routed to the province of the Angels. It was karma; everything had come back to her.

Cain spoke again. "Anything you want, Angelee? Go ahead, you can ask."

"I don't want to be a burden, but do you have anything other than water?" I asked hesitantly.

"We have coffee, and some tea as well."

"What kind of coffee?"

"Black with a bit of milk. There's some milk tea as well. That's it," he said apologetically.

"Tea will be fine, thank you."

"It's served cold. Is that alright?"

"Yes, that's perfectly fine," I said.

He smiled and came back with a whole pitcher of tea, just for me! I knew that must have cost him a fortune. Sierra told me that in her province, products were more expensive than in ours. A tea that cost one dollar in Cosenza would be a dollar fifty in Crotone. It was only fifty cents, yet it added up to a rather large difference. I took small sips, making sure that at least half of the pitcher was left for Sierra and her father.

When I returned the pitcher to him, he shook his head, his eyes fixed on the excess tea. "I don't want people to think we're poor. We're doing our best and making a living. So, finish that tea, because I'll find a way to get more. I work two shifts a day just to earn enough money so that we won't immediately be recognized as Devils. Please don't feel sorry for us because we're less fortunate than you. We have more strength and capability than you would ever imagine. And at the end of the day, that's more valuable than money!" He slammed the pitcher down, clearly frustrated.

Fleur was silent during all this, but her eyes made up for it, expressing everything she was feeling. I, on the other hand, was a person who couldn't leave a conversation half undone. If I didn't apologize, I knew I would feel the guilt.

"I'm sorry." There I sat, saying the two simplest words in existence, not even knowing if it would make up for the disturbance I had caused.

Cain didn't reply. Maybe he wanted something more, and sorry would never be enough.

I spoke again. "I didn't mean to upset you in any way, or to imply that you're less fortunate than me. I'm so single-minded because I grew up in the type of family that doesn't understand what real life is actually like. I've never really experienced that kind of suffering. All I know is that it's bad. So, when I saw you, I just wanted to help. I wanted to save some tea for you, because I know it can be costly. But the truth is, I actually know nothing about your life. And you're right: you guys are so much stronger than me, and you know how to fend for yourselves. So, I apologize, I never wanted to offend you."

Cain shrugged and did his best to form a grin. "Nothing wrong with you trying to help. How we live is not your fault at all. I guess I just wanted you to know that we've got it; we're hanging in there. We appreciate you being considerate, but it just shows that people think Devils aren't strong enough or hardworking enough. We are."

I nodded emphatically, conveying that I understood exactly what he was spelling out, though in reality I never would.

SIERRA

It felt so good to be with my father again, to see his kind eyes and unshaven beard. I hadn't realized how much I'd missed him. He seemed so happy now that I was here. I wondered what the days without me had been like for him. Of course, I had only been at Fleur's for a couple days, but the worst part was that I knew I was going back there, and then to France for who knew how long. That would be only the beginning of my absence in his life, and *his* in mine. It was only going to get worse and worse as time went on. Of course I was excited for the voyage across the Mediterranean Sea, outside the Calabrian borders, but then again, I would feel really homesick. All I had was Calabria and my father and the woods. What if I didn't want to leave them all behind?

The visit to our house went slowly. Fleur and Angelee eventually left, allowing my father and I to sit outside in the setting sun for a while, just the two of us. After some time, he took me to a special outdoor theater built just for the Devils, by a man who catered to our needs without a fee. Everyone knew his name. Since we didn't have access to a big movie screen because electronics were against the law in Calabria, the performance usually included people dancing on the large stage or animals performing unique tricks.

Although it was already dusk, it was hot and sticky outside as we watched the performance. There were no stage lights shining on the performers; the streetlamps provided all the illumination. We kept ourselves cool by spraying water on ourselves, left over from the last rain shower. It felt so good to be with my father, to watch the dancers move gracefully, to hear laughter despite my weariness, to see smiles after I had only seen frowns, to let the sky envelop me in its vibrant coral hues. And no matter how much I tried to make that moment last forever, I knew it would soon come to an end. Life was like that; the good moments only lasted for so long.

Finally, it was night, and I sat on my bed, staring up at the ceiling. What would happen if I couldn't find Fleur's sister? Was she even in France, or was she dead? I didn't know what to believe anymore. I just knew that I had to find Chantelle, to bring her home, for Fleur's sake as well as my own. I had to find her fast, so I could return to my father. How would he fend for himself? I would have to speak to the dictator about that; maybe she could provide him with food for at least a month. And it would mean so much to me if she did; I would get to experience everything I had ever wanted, without worrying about my father.

He was probably fast asleep, right? Good; he deserved to go to bed early. He had taken the day off of work just for me, but tomorrow he would be back at it. I wondered what he could possibly be thinking. Surely, he was anxious about me. On the other hand, my absence would give him peace of mind and allow him to get his work done without stressing. He would be okay. He knew he was going to be okay, and he knew I was going to be okay, just like I knew I was going to be okay.

It was so hard to fall asleep. Tomorrow I would be leaving for France. My bags were all ready. I had packed everything I owned because I knew it would be a long journey. Two long-sleeved shirts for the windy nights, three T-shirts, one sweatshirt, undergarments, toothbrush and toothpaste, other toiletries, and three pairs of socks would be adequate, I thought. Sadly, my whole wardrobe was able to fit in a single suitcase. In the early morning, I would pack the blanket my mother had knitted for me long ago, to give me security and comfort.

What I needed the most was my mother. All this time, I had hidden my sadness from my father, trying to please him, trying to make him happy. But all those days without her, I felt so empty. And even though it had been a little less than a decade since her death, I still could recall her black eyes and gorgeous jet-black hair. I remembered her sweet personality, her sincere smile, and her desire to put others ahead of herself. I would never be able to describe in words how lonely I felt.

She had dreamed of traveling the world: Sri Lanka, Greece, Argentina. Instead of reading a book to me before bedtime when I was little, she would talk to me in whispers. She would promise me, "Sierra, one day you and I will travel the world together. We'll see everything the world has to offer. Calabria is getting boring, don't you think?" And I had believed her—but she had broken her promise.

Traveling to France was what we'd always wanted. I would mend her broken promise. She would look down on me and experience Blesle with me, just as we'd dreamed. That feeling, knowing she was still here with me, tucked in my heart, dried the tears from my cheeks and gave me courage. I was born to leave Calabria. It was everything I had ever wanted. It was everything *we* had ever wanted. This trip was everything. It meant everything.

ANGELEE

It was less awkward on the car ride back than I expected. The chatter between Fleur and me filled most of the empty space. I guessed it was because we could relate to each other so well. We were both wealthy, both from hardworking families, both with a dream that might never be fulfilled, and both considered ungrateful and greedy. Of course there was plenty to talk about.

It took us more than half an hour to get back to Fleur's. As we neared our destination, I noticed a scent of smoke, like a fire left going for too long. There were shouts too—high-pitched screams, and it wasn't just one voice, but many. I knew the dictator could hear, but she kept her lips pursed sternly, her eyes on the road, so I kept silent.

We arrived at the mansion only to be greeted by mobs of people. They flooded the mile-long driveway and stretched out even farther in the opposite direction. Some were carrying torches. Others carried homemade signs: GO TO HELL, or WE SHOULD HAVE FOUGHT BEFORE! Some even said, WE'RE ALL EQUAL, SO PLEASE DON'T MAKE A SEQUEL! People were banging on the car windows, but luckily, they were tinted and bulletproof.

The dictator shouted at me, "I don't want you getting hurt; go hide in the trunk!"

I immediately obeyed, releasing my seat belt and crawling into the back of the car. There were several picnic blankets beneath me, which I slipped over my head as makeshift camouflage. The shouts of protest were getting louder and louder. Strangely, I didn't feel scared; it was like I was in a daze. Was any of this real? An uprising? That had never happened before.

Fleur drove slowly up the driveway, doing her best to avoid the protesters. The bodyguards in the car stayed put, guns raised. Then I heard even more guards come out of the mansion, forcing away the hundreds of people gathered to fight against Fleur and her laws and beliefs. I couldn't see Fleur, but I could feel the pain within her; I could feel her tears. Her whole world was against her. I wanted to give her a big hug, to comfort her like my mother used to comfort me, but I didn't know how.

Fifteen minutes later, when we were all safely within the walls of the mansion, I received a call from Sierra. She was using one of the phones that Fleur had given her so she could contact me during the trip.

"You okay?!" she cried.

"Yeah, I'm fine. Why do you ask?"

"Well, there's a cloud of smoke hovering over my apartment, and when I went outside, I could hear distant shouts."

I sighed. "There's an uprising at the mansion. Hundreds of people are here, angry at Fleur. It doesn't feel real. I mean, it's been so long, and people have always remained silent. I just don't get why they're speaking up now."

"Maybe they know."

"Know what?" I asked.

"Maybe they know that I'm leaving."

"How?"

"I don't know. You didn't tell them, right?" Doubt crept into her voice.

"Sierra, I would never! You know that, right? Could it have been your dad?"

"No, it's not him." Sierra's voice got quiet, but I didn't make much of it.

"Maybe this is about something else. There has to be more to this."

"I don't know. It's just so odd that all of this happened so suddenly," she said.

"Sierra, are you sure that nobody knows about your trip to France?"

Her voice got all quiet again. For a moment, I thought she had hung up.

"I'm positive. No one knows about this trip, except my father. And he wouldn't…" She trailed off, yet I still could make out her shaky breath. I knew she was unsure about something.

We said our goodbyes, and I hung up, not knowing what more to say. I positioned myself at the window that overlooked the Calabrian mountains, then I got in bed and gradually drifted off to sleep.

SIERRA

My dad was the "rooster" of the house. He was the one who called to get me up in the morning, and he was always ready. A breakfast of milk and cereal was waiting for me on the table. He made it special by adding a handful of fresh berries that we grew on the apartment lawn.

"How'd you sleep, cheerio?"

I rolled my eyes. He had called me "cheerio" since my first day of kindergarten. This time I laughed though. "I slept fine. And you?"

He dodged the question, sprinkling some cinnamon on my bowl of cereal.

"How did you sleep?" I repeated.

"I was worried about you. It's sure going to be lonely around here without you."

"Dad, you're working most of the time. You barely see me anyway. It won't make much of a difference."

"I know, I know," he said. "But at least I knew you were here; I knew you were waiting at home for me. Your mother is gone, and even that little calico kitten she used to own. What was her name? Sammy?"

"I'm going to be just fine, and so are you. You don't have to stress about anything. I'll be back before you know it. Plus, I'll have Jia with me." My voice squeaked as I confronted my father with what I had longed to say since last night. "You didn't tell anyone, right? About my trip?"

He shook his head defensively, but didn't say anything more. I took a large gulp and smiled, pretending to believe him, pretending to trust him. He took a seat at the kitchen counter and sipped his coffee slowly.

The whole morning flew by, as if I had only counted to ten. Soon, Angelee and Jia were outside our door, twiddling their thumbs, trying to make the goodbye with my father less awkward. I didn't want to leave my father alone, but we both knew this was the right thing to do.

"Sierra, I'll miss you."

"I know, Father. I'll miss you too." I ran into his arms just as I had done when I was a toddler, and he cradled me until my tears dried. Then he handed me a photograph: my mother, my father, and I against the marvelous backdrop of one of the Calabrian beaches. It was one of the only family photos we had. We looked so nice. My mother was sitting all proper, her hands folded on her skirt. My father had his best button-down on, and his jeans were ironed almost to the point that they looked like they had never been worn before. Mother had dressed me in sunshine-yellow overalls, with a white shirt underneath, identical to hers. A yellow headband was stretched over my hair, and my nails were painted white.

I couldn't accept this photo, no matter how much my father wanted me to take it. I pushed it back into his hands and ran out of the room before he could say anything.

I followed Angelee and Jia all the way down to Fleur's car. Fleur's head was resting on the steering wheel, and her eyes were closed.

Sunlight illuminated her face, making it a peachy tan. Her hair was tousled by the gentle breeze from the open windows. I didn't want to wake her; I knew movies were playing through her head, adventure and love and war. Those dreams must be teaching her, helping her, showing her, giving her some sort of perspective. She was someone else in those dreams, a new individual entirely. Her opinions differed dramatically, her words were sweet rather than harsh, and her life was pleasant rather than a constant battle. I couldn't wake her from those dreams of ease, or she would just enter the nightmare again.

Jia had no such reservations, tapping Fleur gently on the shoulder. Before we knew it, we were back on the road.

"How was it?" Fleur questioned, wondering about my stay with my father.

"It was good. I was happy to see him again."

"Yes, I'm sure," she said.

"So, we're driving to the airport now?"

"We are. See up there, where that small plot of grass meets that road? Just a little ahead of that is the airport."

"Oh. I've never been there before, so I'm not quite familiar with these streets," I said.

"I don't know if you've ever been to the province of Reggio di Calabria, but that's where the airport is."

"No, I've never been to that province. I remember it being closed for a while, but then you opened it up as the trade started coming in and we started forming our own trade routes."

"Yes, yes. It was closed for more than five years," she said. "In fact, I haven't been there for a while either. I found no need to visit it. No tourists come here anymore anyway."

"I think I remember coming to Reggio di Calabria," Angelee cut in. "Summer 2318 or 2319, I forget which one."

"You came with your parents?" This time, Fleur was more attentive.

"No, it was just me," Angelee said.

Jia raised an eyebrow. We were both confused, never imagining that Angelee would sneak out or do anything of that sort.

"Don't be so surprised, you two," she said with a frown, noticing our reactions. "I just needed some space, some time to clear my mind. It's like that sometimes. I just wanted to think, and I wanted to be as far as I could from my parents."

Fleur half smiled, as if to offer reassurance and an apology. "And you took some sort of transportation there by yourself, I presume." She meant the subway, which was quite costly, but ran very smoothly with little disruption. It was a substitute for busses and cars.

"I walked there," Angelee said. "Cosenza and Reggio di Calabria aren't very far apart. My parents had just left for work, and it was after a fight. They wouldn't come back home for at least six hours, so I had time."

By the time our conversation was over, we had arrived at the airport. It was unlike anything I had ever seen before, looming high above the ground, covered with hundreds of big windows. And the airplanes were beautiful, so fragile in their silence.

"Well, I guess this is goodbye for now, then," Fleur said sympathetically, but I could tell she was faking it.

"Goodbye?" I answered, obviously confused.

"You don't have to check in or anything. Aeroporto dello Stretto is a small airport, and as the dictator, I have every right to tell those flight attendants what to do.”

“So, this is it, then?”

“This is it,” she replied as we stepped out of the car.

Angelee and Jia shared a small frown. But Fleur came first; I guessed she wanted to get it over with.

“Sierra, we’ll miss you. And I can’t thank you enough for traveling to France. My sister means the world to me, and if she’s still alive, I wouldn’t know what to say. If you have any questions at all, just give me a call using that little phone I gave you. But I’m sure you’ll be fine, and it will be the adventure of a lifetime. We’ll check in on your father, provide him with all the food he needs. He’ll be okay, and so will you.” And even though she came over to give me a hug, her posture remained as stiff as her starched skirt. “And here, you can have this. It’s for when you take off and land. Your ears may feel strange, so just suck on this.” She handed me a couple candies. I slid them into my pocket and thanked the dictator for everything she had done.

Finally, Angelee came over. I guessed she didn’t want to cry in front of all of us. In truth, I really wouldn’t have minded. I just wanted someone to love me, the way I had loved my mother.

“Sierra, I’m sorry.”

“Why do you keep saying that? You’ve already apologized, over and over again.”

“I can’t help but feel guilty.”

“There’s nothing to feel guilty about, trust me,” I reassured her.

“I know, I know.” Despite her best efforts, her tears came flowing out. “We’ve only known each other a few days, but you’ve become like my sister. You’ve taught me so many things that I didn't even know about myself, and you've changed me. I wish I could come, but I know you two will have fun. Jia, please take care of Sierra. Hopefully I'll get to see you both soon though. Tell me everything, guys—about the trees, and the skies, and the food. Remember me."

"We will." I smiled as we locked pinkies.

The airplane was much larger than I'd expected, and it soared like a bird. The pilot didn't come out to greet us, like we had both wanted, and the ride was rather turbulent, but the view from the window made up for all of it. I had been on the ground my whole life, held captive within borders I had never hoped to break through. And then all at once, I was on top of everything. I was free, my chains broken, my wings finally found. Everything had instantly become so small below. The trees that had once towered above me were the size of a crumb. And I felt big—bigger than the people down there. Looking at Jia, I knew she felt the same way.

Blesle was in south central France, and it would take approximately one hour to get there. The only passengers were Jia and me. The aisle was narrow, but wide enough for a slim cart to come rolling through. The flight attendant handed Jia a slim glass of juice, per her request. Then she asked if I would care for a drink, offering me a selection of juices or sparkling water. I shook my head; I wanted neither.

The peaceful clouds, the deep blue outside, and the hum of the engine all made me tired, and I dozed off.

I awoke to Jia tapping me, urging me to wake up. I stared out the window. As we descended, all the trees and buildings began to enlarge until everything looked lifelike once more. An hour had passed, perhaps a little more, but I wasn't keeping track. It must have been close to noon, as the sun hung high in the sky. I could tell almost immediately that France looked different than

Italy, with quaint cottages closely knit together. We were nearing the runway; only thirty miles until landing. My ears felt clogged, and my heart was racing. I dug in my pocket for one of the sour candies Fleur had given me and stuffed it into my mouth. The landing was easy after that. My ears no longer throbbed, and my anticipation was building.

It just felt so surreal, like a dream. I was the one chosen. Of all the people who lived in Calabria, I was chosen to be in the heart of France. What more could any person want? The seat belt sign illuminated, and I felt as if I were falling in slow motion from the sky above. Even when I was back on the ground, I still felt on top of the world.

I had once known my limits. I had known I had to stay within the borders of Calabria. I had known I could never leave, even if I wanted to. But here I was, fourteen hundred miles from home. Fourteen hundred miles away from everything I had ever known.

ANGELEE

Once we dropped Sierra and Jia off at the airport, Fleur and I drove back to her mansion. Time passed slowly and quietly. However, dinner came quickly, and after eating, I requested that Fleur drop me off at Scilla beach. I told her I needed to clear my mind, and oddly, she agreed.

The waves skimmed my feet. I waded further in until it was up to my knees. The ocean seemed so perfect on the surface. It could turn dead fish into beautiful coral. Maybe that was why I longed to be by the ocean; it took something so ugly, like the emotions inside of me, and turned them into something pleasant.

The boats were docked to my left, and the houseboat was just a little bit beyond that. I wished I knew how to drive a boat. If I did, I would have been gone a long time ago. But I could go now, I thought. No one was here to stop me. After all, this could be my last chance. My parents would be coming to pick me up very soon after their vacation came to an end. The waves were calling me, and the boats all lined up symmetrically were everything I could ask for. This was my chance, and I had been waiting for this moment all my life.

But for some reason, my feet stayed where they were, my body frozen. I didn't know what was keeping me from leaving. Maybe it was my family. No matter how much my mind wanted to leave them behind, my heart could never do it.

The wind tore through me, and everything seemed so unfamiliar. I knew I would hate myself for not leaving, but I would also hate myself *for* leaving. My gut was telling me not to take that risk, to just return to my normal life.

Maybe nature was mad at me too for choosing not to leave, because it started raining—the kind of rain that stung. Or maybe the rain was actually a warning, telling me I shouldn't go. I couldn't go. I *wouldn't* go.

After what seemed like forever, I found myself back on the houseboat. I had stayed inside my comfort zone for my whole life. I had only ever lived in my parents' ideal world, but that could only go on for so long. Sometimes you had to leave in order to find your own world. *Go, go, go!*

I clasped the steering wheel, and the cool brown leather felt so good in my hands.

"Angelee? Angelee!" Fleur hollered at the top of her lungs, hoping that her voice would somehow find its way to me. My face flushed pink with panic, and my hands were trembling. She wouldn't find me here—at least, I hoped not. I wiped my clammy hands on my pants and then clung to the steering wheel. She was getting closer; it was now or never, I told myself.

Ahead of me was a large glass window that displayed a full view of Scilla beach. Blacks and blues and everything in between stretched across the sky. The moon was mirrored in the water, even more beautiful than the stars surrounding it. The waves moved silently, smoothly. Oh, how I wished I could stare at those waves forever.

The dictator's increasingly frantic cries brought me back to reality. Fleur was getting closer and closer to finding me. I searched for a key to start the engine. I could hear doors slamming on empty ships, echoing in the silence. Finally, I found the key in an unlocked safe. Without hesitation, I cranked the engine, hoping she wouldn't hear it.

But she did.

SIERRA

I recalled the dictator saying that Blesle was a small town. Its population was barely a thousand people. The town seemed to be bustling though. All kinds of people were scurrying about, carrying books and baskets, gossiping, giggling, and shouting. I tried to find my way through the crowd. We were in the heart of Blesle, in the town square. The streets were lined with aged cobblestones, and rose bushes bordered the stone walls.

Blesle was located in central France, home to the rolling hills typical of the French countryside. As Jia and I walked further and further north, the crowd gradually died down, almost to the point where we could hear ourselves breathe. Almost every house we walked by had an orange roof. Back home, the apartments in the south end of our courtyard stood tall, four or five stories high. But the houses in Blesle were larger in size, painted white just like the streetlamps, more wide than tall. Even so, they left a lot of room for land. The houses were spaced out with what seemed like a half mile between them.

"I guess we just walk from here?" Jia wondered.

"Fleur didn't give us an address. She just suggested we stay at the main hotel here. Let's just walk until we find some food first. My stomach is growling right now."

"I thought you'd be used to not eating much, after all those nights

"

of going hungry," she observed.

"Well, now that I have an opportunity to eat, it's all I can think about."

And that was all we said for a while. The cobblestone streets turned into dirt paths, which was a struggle for our rolling suitcases, and the houses slowly disappeared. The mountains surrounded Jia and me on either side. Between them, hills and valleys rolled on for what seemed like ages. The dirt path seemed to continue endlessly, but the sun was now setting, and the wind was cold. My throat stung from the frigid air surrounding us. We were both exhausted from the adrenaline of this journey, so we sat down on the path. I sat cross-legged and took long, deep breaths.

"All Fleur said was to find the main hotel here," Jia said. "It's my fault we've come so far. I should've thought to ask someone in the town square."

"It's fine. I'm sure we'll come across it soon," I murmured with false hope.

"Maybe we should just camp here for the night. It would be better than walking even farther," Jia sighed.

"No, I'm starving. We both need food right now."

"Okay, fine. Let's continue. We have to hurry though; it's almost nighttime."

Pleased with Jia's decision to keep walking north, I calmed myself down, reminding myself that good things would be coming soon.

Then up ahead, a figure emerged from the twilight, dressed in black. It appeared to be coming closer, singing a haunting tune. It sounded less like a song and more like a warning. Darkness was falling around us, and the first stars could finally be seen in the absence of the sun.

The figure was coming closer and closer. A black veil covered their head, but I could make out the outline of their lips and the gleam of their eyes. A demon, a devil—that was what they looked like. I should know, because I was one too. But they were a different type of devil than me—the powerful type, with the resources of an Angel, but the intentions of a stereotypical Devil.

ANGELEE

I was out on the water before anybody could stop me. I wasn't even thinking about whether I had made the right decision or not. All I was thinking about was how I would escape successfully. But the moment I started the engine, the moment I took off, I felt an uneasy feeling in the pit of my stomach. It wasn't guilt; it was regret.

I had only been on the water for less than twenty minutes before bright headlights appeared behind me, trying to track me down. Anxious and fearful, I closed my eyes and pushed the throttle all the way forward. The boat surged through the waves. It was very hard to control, though I was sure that if I hadn't been the one driving, the ride would have been perfectly smooth.

Just then, lightning struck, thunder crashed, and rain started pouring down. In that moment, I realized how much I had taken those sunny, blue-skied days at the vineyard for granted, those smiles I had shared with my family. I missed those days where happiness was around the corner, when the Earth was bright and alive. I missed those days where I was excited to grow up, so undaunted by the future.

A few hours later, the storm was dying down. I had successfully outrun the boats chasing me. But I realized I still needed a plan. I had finally put everything into perspective. I had no source of food or water. The only communication I had with land was through the cell phone Fleur had given me. I was stranded at sea, with nowhere to go, but nowhere to be. My family had no idea of my whereabouts. A search team had been looking for me, but I had lost sight of them a long time ago. I only had myself for company.

There were more questions than answers. How was I going to survive? What would I do at night? Would I leave Calabria for the rest of my life? Where would I go? How would I make a living? The only reasonable answer that came to mind was to go back home. If I just turned the houseboat around, everything would go back to normal.

Great, I thought to myself, *another hard decision*. In truth, it was similar to the last choice I'd made: should I stay or go? But this time, the answer mattered even more. I wanted to halt the boat in its path, just so I could have some time to think.

I continued at a slow and steady pace. My eyes were on the water ahead, but my mind was elsewhere. What would my life look like if I chose to continue with this journey? I would probably never go back to Calabria; the shame of leaving in the first place would be enough embarrassment. I would most definitely stay somewhere in northern Italy, in case my parents came to find me. No matter how much I thought I despised them, I knew I would be dead if they hadn't adopted me.

In northern Italy, I would find a job. I would have no choice. Maybe I would work at an office, or a gelato shop, or on the canals. But what would my life turn out to be like if I went back home? Honestly, it would just be the same as before. I would plead with Fleur not to spill the secret that I had attempted to leave. I would go back to those boring days of school and sit by the vineyard and pretend to laugh at my friends' jokes.

My sense of adventure was enough to persuade me. I knew the

risk I was willing to take.

SIERRA

$\mathbf{A}$ faint whiff of banana bread and oat milk wafted up toward the loft. White flakes pranced down from the gray clouds. It was unusual to have snow in the summer, especially in this part of France.

The loft in which Jia and I were staying was on the upper floor of a cottage in the French countryside. The house belonged to none other than the figure in the black veil. It was beautiful and airy. The home was layered with plush carpets and macramé pillows, and there were candles everywhere. Like the others we had observed, the house was built with more width than height. It had only two floors, but they stretched wide. The bottom floor had a kitchen, sitting room, washroom, and dining room. The loft upstairs was one large room, containing no walls, which meant a lot of extra space. It was plain and simple, carpeted in a fuzzy gray material. There were three queen-sized beds all lined up on one wall. Even though the house wasn't too big, miles of open terrain surrounded it, fields of flowers and evergreen trees, with many square acres for animals to roam.

I stared at Jia's bed, which was right next to mine. Hers was empty, and so was the other one. I sat up, rubbed my eyes, and stumbled my way down the stairs.

The woman had taken off her black veil and sat snugly at the kitchen table with a mug cupped in her hands. Jia was positioned on the kitchen counter, occupying herself with a piece of buttered toast.

"Oh, you're awake! My name is Romily," the woman said in awkward English. "Uh … good morning! I invited you into my home last night. So now, tell me what it is you came here for."

When I saw that Jia was stuffing food in her mouth, I took it as a signal that she didn't feel like speaking, so I did. "Well, I come from Calabria, Italy, and she comes from China. My dictator is searching for her sister, who she believed was dead. But there have been some rumors that her sister was seen here, so she sent us to see what we could find out."

"Oh, I see." Romily looked down at the kitchen floor, clearly wondering what to say next. She seemed petrified, and I wasn't sure why. "And why exactly would her sister be here?"

"Well, the dictator, Fleur, grew up here. But when she moved to Calabria, her sister stayed here in Blesle. The two siblings haven't seen each other in a long time, so Fleur doesn't know if she's still alive, or if that's just a lie."

"So, do you have any idea what this sister of hers looks like?" Romily asked as she brushed a strand of fiery red hair out of her face.

"Fleur gave us a picture of her. It's packed away in my suitcase. Her name is Chantelle."

"Alright, alright. I was just asking because last night, I didn't get a chance to meet you. I'll help you find her after breakfast. Until then, why don't you eat something, Sierra?"

I couldn't remember whether or not I had told her my name. Maybe Jia had introduced me.

"Thank you, but I'm not that hungry," I said..

She smirked. "Don't be shy. What would you like?"

"Anything is fine," I said quietly.

Breakfast was a tall glass of oat milk and soft pancakes stacked high, drizzled with maple syrup. Romily sat at the table with us. I felt a great sense of tranquility in that moment, sitting there in the morning sun, with a full belly and not a care in the world. If I had to be honest, my thoughts were not focused on home. I knew my father was okay, and I surprisingly didn't miss Angelee as much as I had expected. I had called her last night with the phone Fleur had given me. She seemed anxious, but I didn't give it much thought. I told her I missed her, and she told me that she missed me even more. But I didn't miss her the way I said. And in truth, I didn't feel bad about that.

ANGELEE

My hands had been gripping the steering wheel for hours. I hadn't slept at all. At times, I would have to force my eyes to stay open, and that task was arduous in itself.

All I had was some money from my parents' safe, which I always had on me. I had no food and no water. I had no closure either; I hadn't even said goodbye to my parents. I hadn't said goodbye to the room that I grew up in. I hadn't said goodbye to the vineyard. How could I leave behind the things I loved most, without so much as a farewell?

Today will be different though, I thought as I prepared to sleep. I would drive the boat for a couple of hours and grab lunch somewhere on land with my parents' money. Then I would get back on the water, drive some more, eat some leftover lunch, dock again, and sleep. And in about a week, I would be exactly where I wanted to be: central Italy. Naples, to be exact.

It almost seemed like a dream to me. It was all finally happening, and so quickly. I was free. Free from the dictator. Free from Calabria. Free from my parents. Free from sadness.

The sky looked red today. Having grown up by the sea, I knew the old fishermen's saying: "Red sky at night, sailors delight; red sky in the morning, sailors take warning." I groaned with frustration. Yet another storm was on the horizon. It probably wouldn't be safe to drift on the water while a storm was brewing. So, I made the quick decision to stop for the night. I docked the boat at the nearest dock I could find.

Tiny droplets of rain fell from the sky, lightly at first, then heavily. I was on deck with no umbrella; everything from my hair down to my socks was soaked. I decided to leave the boat and come back soon. I sprinted along the wooden dock that led to the town of Palermo. I had taken the boat around the toe of Italy's boot and was now coming back up the west coast. It would be a long journey to Naples; I was less than one fourth of the way there.

Palermo was just as beautiful as Calabria, if not more so. It was surrounded by blue water, and the mountains surrounding it were even more blue. The houses were stacked up the mountains, hidden amidst the peaks. The main street, Via Roma, was lined with golden buildings that shimmered in the sunlight. Several shops lined the street, but most of it was taken up by historical statues and buildings.

Up ahead, a small girl, probably six or seven years old, handed a woman a paper menu. The woman didn't even stop. The girl had overgrown bangs covering her eyes and a tired, sad face. As I approached, she handed me a menu too, but she was still trying to make herself small, concealing herself behind an arch.

I thanked her and smiled. "Do you know where this restaurant is?" I questioned in a soft voice.

The girl pointed further down the street and resumed handing out menus. I hurried under the arches, which provided shelter from the ongoing rain.

The café was small, tucked away, a hidden gem. Warm and quiet, it had orange walls and cream tiled floors. The windows were plastered with hundreds of advertisements and posters. In truth, it wasn't a proper café, but more like a diner. The leather seats were gradually wearing away, and the air smelled of spoiled milk. I was too hungry to care about the waiter's unprofessional manner. I ordered three bowls of salad and bread for the boat ride, as I wouldn't be stopping again for food for a while. The waiter took my money and waved me off, even though she had no other customers to serve.

Back inside, the boat was warm, and I was protected from the heavy rainstorm. I put the boat in gear and set off once again.

SIERRA

Romily led me to the stable outside of her house.

"These horses are so beautiful, aren't they?" From the way she talked about them and the way she smiled when she told us their names, I could tell she had a passion for them.

"Yes, they are," Jia and I said in unison. I grinned, marveling at their silky manes.

"They've helped me a lot. I was an orphan; my parents died from an illness at a young age. But my foster mother owned a horse, and I used to ride it every day. She gave me riding lessons, and these horses became my friends. They gave me back everything that had been taken away from me." She nodded. It was a nod filled with pain, but hope too, as if all the nostalgia were flooding back to her.

"And this is the stable boy, Ackerley," she said as a thin boy walked in. He wore a straw hat that cast a shadow over half of his face, and tattered clothes that hung loosely on his body. "I'll be away for a while, running some errands in town, so he'll guide you around while I'm gone. He's the best we've had for a long time, so I trust that you're in good hands." With that, she headed back to the house before going out.

Ackerley blushed and shifted his eyes toward the ground.

"Hi," Jia said awkwardly.

"Hello," Ackerley said with a dim smile.

"Well, we were wondering if you could help us find a woman named Chantelle?" Jia asked.

"Yeah, I know," he said plainly, his emotions absent.

"Great," I muttered.

"What?" he asked, confused by my sarcasm.

"I was just hoping to stay in France a little longer," I explained. "I've barely gotten to see it."

"No worries, you'll see it soon enough. Plus, I've heard from… from others that Chantelle isn't easy to deal with. So, trust me, you won't be leaving any time soon." He grinned slyly.

"What do you mean by that?" Jia asked—the same thing I was wondering.

"She's a stubborn one, to say the least. The type of person who always wants things their way," Ackerley responded.

"Okay," I cut in. "First, we have to figure out where she lives."

Ackerley was hidden in the shadows. A patch of sun was only a few feet in front of him, but he chose to stay in the dark. Maybe he wanted the shade and the cold, but I could tell that it was something much deeper, as if he were hiding a secret in the shadows.

ANGELEE

It was dark out again. The storm had finally dissipated, and the air was clear again. The boat was docked somewhere near Messina, which was opposite Reggio di Calabria. I ate the leftover salad and bread, taking small bites so I would have enough to last.

Although I had plenty of my parents' money, it would probably still not be enough to cover my expenses until I found a job in Naples, which could take a long time. I would have to rent a small apartment, and I would need money for transport, food and beverages, clothes, hygiene products… The list went on.

A sudden buzzing interrupted my thoughts. Oh no! Fleur was calling my cell phone, and her name on the screen made my heart drop. On first instinct, I picked up. Wrong decision. What was I thinking?

"Where are you?!" she demanded.

"Home. I'm home," I replied sternly, trying to keep my voice from breaking.

Fleur cursed quietly, away from the speaker, before hollering back, "I was scared to death! Your parents were supposed to pick you up today. Why did you choose to go home so soon? I could've called your parents yesterday, explaining that you were already home. Now they're on their way to pick you up."

"No!" I shrieked, my anxiety building. "Tell them to go in the other direction."

"Angelee," she said haughtily, "your parents are coming here, no matter what. Now it's up to me to make the decisions. I can barely trust you anymore. I'm not even sure if you *are* at home. I heard something by the boats last night, and I saw a slender silhouette. If you dared to escape, you'd better come back today! This is your last chance before you get punished. You don't have a choice."

But she was wrong. I did.

"You have nothing to worry about. I'm okay," I tried to reassure Fleur. But it didn't quite work, because at the same time, I needed to reassure myself. "I'm at home, safe and sound," I said quietly.

I immediately hung up the phone. Then another call came in. It was my parents.

SIERRA

Jia and I exchanged worried glances as Ackerley led us up the narrow hillside. A dark forest was up ahead. Tall trees with long branches lined the dirt path, and the sun was hidden by the dark green leaves.

A sign with big red letters was secured to a metal fence. "'Private property. Do not enter,'" Jia read. "Great, just what we need."

"Don't worry," the stable boy assured her, "we're traveling in the right direction. We're going to stop by Romily's moms' house. She passed two weeks ago, unfortunately, but she has information about everyone and everything in her records. Romily said we can go into her house. We could probably find something in there."

I went first, staying on the dirt path, keeping an eye out for poison ivy or harmful insects. I kept my eyes on the ground the entire time. Jia and Ackerley followed, all three of us holding hands. It was scary. I had never been anywhere outside of Calabria. But here I was in a strange forest, with two virtual strangers. All I had was myself, in a new country across the Tyrrhenian Sea. I knew everything happened for a reason, but I was still trying to figure out mine. Why was I in France? Why was I with Ackerley and Jia? Why had I been born in such a harsh region? I didn't know.

We went on like that for at least twenty minutes. The forest was intimidating. I had never seen trees like these before; they were so thick that I could barely see through them. But the forest was just as magical as it was haunting. It was so alive—birds chirping, insects humming, water rippling. All my life, I'd thought the whole world was a terrible place, but that was just *my* world. Ackerley's world and Jia's world seemed so free. How could you think poorly of your world when you got to visit beautiful places every day? How could you feel alone when your surroundings were so *alive*?

Soon, the green of the forest began to die off and melt into soft browns, and the dirt path became a smooth paved road. The birds, and insects faded into the background.

Romily's mother's cottage, covered with strands of ivy, stood alone in the distance. As we approached, a scream suddenly erupted from the house. No—from *outside* the house. It was full of terror and pain.

ANGELEE

"Where are you?!" my mother cried on the phone.

"I'm home." My breath shook as I tried to enunciate the words. I tried to pretend that what I was saying was real.

My mother didn't believe it. "Don't lie to me! Fleur just called us while we were on the way to her house. She said you were home, so we turned around and checked every single room in the house. Even the vineyard! You're nowhere to be found."

"I'm fine."

"Where *are* you?" my mother pleaded. "This isn't like you, Angelee. I'm stressed out as it is… We'll have to call the police if you don't explain to me right this second what has gotten into you!"

It was partly her fault that I had run away, yet I was the one getting blamed for it? Before I had time to react, my father stole the phone from my mother and comforted her with a gentle whisper: "It's okay, she'll come back to us."

I imagined my mother faking a smile, pretending that she was okay, pretending that she was strong. But in reality, she was not. She probably felt like breaking down, falling on the floor and crying. At the same time, she probably felt rage building up inside of her. And if I came back, if I were to run into her arms again, would she tear me down and scream at me for leaving? Or would she love me again and tell me everything would be okay? I knew the answer—and it was telling me not to go back.

"Angelee, you're freaking us out," my father said. "Come back—*please* come back. I made a promise to your mother. I told her that you would be here. Don't make me break that promise. Come home. It's lonely here without you." Suddenly it got very quiet, until he said, "Whatever made you decide to leave?"

I didn't feel like lying anymore; the guilt was too heavy. "It was my choice, my decision." All at once, I felt like a child again, explaining to my father why I'd gotten in a fight with a girl at school, or why I'd painted on the walls. I felt embarrassed and afraid. "But I'm sticking with it."

"Honey, please. Tell me the truth."

"I *am* telling you the truth!" I shouted into the phone. Finally, everything that had been bottled up inside me for years was coming out. "Why can't you just accept it? I'm gone. I'm *gone!* I'm gone," I repeated. "And it's all your fault."

SIERRA

Ackerley smiled as I stared in shock. He was just letting it all happen. He was letting the girl scream, letting her die before his eyes. The worst part was that he didn't bother to do anything about it.

The girl was struggling, her black hair spilling down to her shoulders. She only looked a few years old. She wore clothes that blended in with the earth around her. Her eyes were shut as she lay on her back, arms and legs strewn out to the sides. Expertly knotted ropes were tied around her body, making it so that she was unable to move. There seemed to be no life in her. I foraged around, hoping to find a sharp enough stick to cut the rope and set her free. Jia was doing the same, panicking and gulping in short, quick breaths.

We both paid little attention to Ackerley; we were too anxious to wonder what had gotten into him. He continued smiling obliviously. But when I looked into his eyes, I sensed more fear than cruelty. He was hiding something, trying to conceal it behind that awful grin.

Small drops of blood erupted from my finger; I must have poked it on something. I explored the ground beneath me, only to find that a pointy stick had jabbed me. Carefully, I grabbed it and poked and prodded at the girl, attempting to cut the ropes. I checked for a pulse, pressing my fingers against her wrist. Sure enough, there was still some life in her. Jia managed to find a sharp stick too, and we gradually freed the girl from her bonds. In a way, it reminded me of myself; I was finally free from the ties that had held me captive.

Once the rope was undone, I gathered a handful of frigid water from a nearby stream and doused the girl with it. But she didn't wake up—not after the second pour of water, and not after the third. She stayed put, eyes closed, heartbeat waning.

ANGELEE

Why did I have the nerve to say such a cruel thing like that? How was it that easy for me to tear someone apart?

Messina was quiet. There was no movement or action. People were docked in their houses, just as I was docked in the harbor. But Messina offered just what I needed: peace and quiet. Time to think. Time to reflect. Time to mourn. Time to dream.

All that was left in me was numbness, and apart from that, fear. It seemed as if all the lights had turned off, and the whole world had gone dark. I was alone, with no one to save me or protect me from the dangerous things lurking in the shadows. I couldn't move. I couldn't breathe. There was nothing left inside me, nothing to fill my hollowness. I was truly and utterly alone, stuck at sea with no one to hold me. And this time, more than ever before, I felt completely stranded. At home, at least I had some comfort from my parents. But here, they had no idea where I was. I had no one to go back to, nowhere to travel, and nothing in between. My only options were to keep moving or stay put. But I couldn't back down now. I was the type of person who felt dissatisfied if I didn't finish something I had started. So, I would have to keep going, pushing until all the strength was drained out of my system.

But first … sleep. I needed that more than anything. My eyes shut, and the world swallowed me. Everything became dark, and the only company I had was my dreams. In an instant, I was sucked into a realm of unfamiliar memories and distant moments.

I was barely breathing, my nightmares choking me. I could barely hear or see, and when I woke up, my throat was pierced with a sharp stabbing, my stomach was cramping with pain, and my mind was spinning. My vision was distorted, my equilibrium totally off. The fact that I had never been on a boat before was probably why I felt so ill.

It was unlike me to become ill. My mother was a big believer in everything medical, as her own mother had been a doctor. We had the money, so we made a point to prioritize our healthcare. Whenever we had a chance to go to the doctor, we would, whether to receive doses of the latest vaccine or pills that prevented cancer. My mother was odd; she thought of medicine as a trend that everyone should follow. She always wanted to keep up with the latest medical articles and journals. So, it was unusual that I wasn't on top of my well-being. But it was most likely because my mother wasn't here.

I missed them—missed them a lot. But what would it matter if I went back?

SIERRA

"So, how'd it happen?" I asked in my calmest voice, so it wouldn't frighten her.

"J'ai été laissé ici," the girl said. She was thankfully alive and finally awake. She remained calm, but was on the verge of crying. I didn't understand her French one bit, but I tried to reassure her in Italian, hoping that she would somehow take some meaning from my words, as the languages were quite similar.

"Non preoccuparti, lo scopriremo." ("Don't worry, we'll figure it out.")

"I speak fluent French. I could help," offered Ackerley.

A sigh of relief washed over me. At least he was useful for something.

"Je suis venu avec Maman. Elle m'a laissé ici. Elle m'a dit qu'elle revenait."

"She's saying she came here with her mother, and she was left alone here. Her mother told her she would come back. I guess she never did," Ackerley translated.

After some more translation, we finally figured it out. There was a woman who had come while the girl's mother was away, red-haired and evil. The woman had tied the little girl up, but we didn't know why. The little girl had just been minding her business and licking an orange lollipop. So, who was the redhead? And why had she harmed a little girl when the girl had done nothing to deserve it?

ANGELEE

After minutes of me calling with no answer, Sierra finally decided to pick up.

"Where were you?" I demanded.

"I have a life too, you know," Sierra muttered.

"I know, I know."

"You're sitting at home, but I actually have things to do." I couldn't tell whether she was fighting with me in a joking way or in a real way.

"For the record, it wasn't my choice to stay home! And … I'm not home anymore, anyway."

"What do you mean?" Sierra asked.

"I'm in the houseboat. I escaped, and now I'm in Messina," I responded.

"What?! I thought you said you were going to wait for me when I came back. You promised me!"

"I thought that plan was long gone. I'm sorry, I really am, but this is for the best. We're each on our own paths. Maybe one day, our paths will cross again," I told her.

"So, this is it, then? This is the end?" Sierra sighed.

"No, this isn't the end. We'll keep in contact."

"How many promises are you going to break?"

"We'll see each other again, I promise. This isn't the end. And this is a promise I can keep wholeheartedly," I assured her.

"So, see you soon, then?

"See you soon. Destiny will bring us together again, just like it did in the beginning."

And then we hung up. I reflected that most people wouldn't even consider Sierra and me to be friends. We were completely different people with completely different lives. We had only met each other a few days ago. Yet it still felt like she was my sister, and even if we were miles apart, we would still love each other. That's what they said, right? Absence makes the heart grow fonder. Distance could make the heart ache bitterly, but when the distance ended, all of that pain would leave.

We were a few thousand miles apart. But that didn't matter. The distance was temporary, but our friendship was permanent.

SIERRA

The girl was gone; her mother *had* come back for her. But now that one problem was solved, there was still another to deal with. Ackerley was pushing us away from the cottage, fists clenched and ready to fight.

"Ackerley, let us in! We need to find some sort of records on Chantelle's whereabouts!" Jia shouted. I had never seen her get mad before, but when she did, she meant it.

There was silence as the stable boy tried to come up with some excuse for keeping us out of the house.

"Just listen, please. Romily's in there. She just texted me; it's only been thirteen days since her mother's death. A soul supposedly lingers in the air for thirteen days. This is the last day that her mother is around, and she's just paying a little tribute. She wants to keep it private."

"Oh, I had no idea. She didn't seem down about it," Jia whispered.

"Romily has a way of hiding her emotions. But the reason she wanted to run errands was to get some flowers for her mother," Ackerley stated.

He was clearly proud that even he believed his own lie. But I wasn't going to fall for it like Jia had. I knew something was up. Something was definitely off with both Romily and Ackerley.

We waited and waited, crouching on the pebbled road surrounding the cottage. Flower beds of carnations and sunshine-yellow tulips dotted the grassy fields that acted as a backdrop. The sun was no longer beating down on us; instead, the snow drifted down once again, despite the season. None of us talked to each other. We just played with the pebbles, rolling them back and forth in our palms. It was a long wait—longer than any of us expected. I didn't know whether to believe Ackerley, but if Romily's mother had died, then it was only right to wait as long as we had to. Ackerley told us that Romily was in her mother's cottage, grieving.

But Romily never came out. Not after half an hour, or even after an hour.

ANGELEE

The rain was long gone, and the water was quite pleasant, a marvelous cyan. The breeze was gentle, and no clouds dotted the sky. It would be a good day, I told myself.

Once, when I was little, I had come up with a theory that I thought to be true for everyone. If you had a good morning, you would have a bad afternoon. If you had a good day, tomorrow would be terrible. Basically, the good always found a way to balance out the bad, and vice versa. Therefore, since yesterday had been terrible, today would hopefully be better. But you couldn't always predict things like that. Your hopes would get ruined, and things would turn out in the way you least expected. So, I prayed and prayed. *Please let this be a good day; I can't handle the bad anymore. I want my little piece of sunshine. I'm sick of storms. Let the sky be light. Please, please, please…*

I was still docked in Messina, hoping to get to Catanzaro, or even better, Tropea. Those two places were on the west coast of Italy, but much farther south than I was hoping to live. Naples was a while away, which meant there was still a long distance to travel.

The days flew by in a blur, one after the other. They all seemed the same. I would wake up, get ready, and have a small bite to eat (usually toast and jam, or whatever I purchased when I was docked). I would drive the boat for hours, and then I would find dinner wherever I was docked. Finally, I would drift off to sleep, letting the ocean's currents lull me into slumber. Then everything would repeat.

It only took me one day to get to Tropea from Messina. The journey from Tropea to Salerno was a longer journey though, taking two-and-a-half days. Salerno was just south of Naples, so it took less than half a day to finally arrive. My total journey from Calabria to Naples had taken a little less than a week. With a high-powered and expensive boat like the one I was piloting, I would've thought that it would take much less than that. But there were times when I stayed put, like when I felt sick, or had to eat, or had to talk with Sierra or my parents or Fleur. My parents had sent boats out to look for me, but I was already so far out that they couldn't catch up.

People said the journey was what mattered. But for me, the destination was all that counted. I was finally here, in Naples, Italy.

SIERRA

I couldn't take it anymore. It was already dusk, and we could barely see the sun anymore. The flurries moved slowly, the ground completely carpeted in a white fuzz. Snow was unusual here, but with climate change, odd weather occurrences had become frequent. The cold swallowed me whole, removing all the warmth left within me. Everything was darkening. Finally, all the lights turned off, and the sky became a velvety pitch black.

Jia was sitting on the snowy pebbles. She didn't say anything. She didn't want to be the bad guy and ruin Romily's "prayer." But I knew better. This was my chance—my *only* chance. We had come here for a reason: to solve the mystery, to bring back Chantelle. I wasn't just going to sit around all day while Romily cried. I didn't even believe that her mother had really died. But if she had, Romily would just have to suck it up and swallow her tears.

All of a sudden, I was on my feet. I ran towards the front door of the cottage. I was angry—angry that Romily wasn't strong enough to process death. I had been so very young when my mother died. But I processed it, got right back on my feet, and kept going. Why couldn't Romily do the same?

When I walked into the cottage, I almost fainted. In the darkness, I saw an old woman, holding a cane in her left hand. She was lying on the floor, surrounded by a pool of blood, so red it made me sick. Romily was standing just beyond her, and Ackerley too.

She appeared unfazed; she didn't know I was there. Ackerley was crouched down, holding a paper towel sopping with blood.

Romily had injured the young girl by the cottage.

Romily had killed this elderly woman.

ANGELEE

Now what? I thought. I was finally here, in Naples. I was standing at the port, my suitcase brushing my leg. I just stood there for a while, marveling at the beauty, marveling at how far I had come. It was a dream, wasn't it?

What would I do though? I hadn't come here for nothing. I had come here for some excitement, for something new. The only thing I could really do was walk forward, head high, chest broad. I had to be confident.

There were a number of people crowding the streets, holding babies, holding hands, holding ice cream. There were so many people, so many new faces. Back home in Calabria, I knew almost everyone, as I had seen them my whole life. In Naples, everyone was a stranger. But I was not intimidated. In fact, I was invigorated. No one knew my name.

I slept in the Giardini Botanici di Napoli that night. It was a famous park in the heart of Naples, filled with lots of beautiful vegetation. No wonder the gardens were always filled with tourists. As the night began to fall, the crowd lessened. I finally got to see the beauty of the gardens, how the green leaves were highlighted in the silver moonlight, and how the vibrant flowers stood tall in the dark soil. I looked for a place to rest, at least for tonight. I was sick of sleeping on the houseboat. I would rather be on land, surrounded by the excitement of a new and unfamiliar place.

I eventually positioned myself on a park bench, yanked a knitted blanket out of my suitcase, and carefully laid it out on the bench. This makeshift bed would be just fine, yet still I longed for the luxury of my queen bed back home. I situated my hands under my head, so I could lie on my back and stare at the glittering stars. Everything was quiet; the only sound I could hear was the cicadas singing a lullaby. The streetlamps soon illuminated, providing a certain solace, just like my nightlight back home.

On either side of the park bench were gravel paths that held an abundant amount of plants. Every species had a label, from small yellow flowers to cactuses. The dense trees above me shaded my face from the drizzle. Almost as soon as I closed my eyes, I fell asleep.

I woke up to the sun's blazing heat on my tanned skin. Perhaps it wasn't the sun that had woken me up, or the chirping of the birds, but the park ranger standing in front of me. I was too sleepy to even understand what was happening. I could barely make out his features, as my eyes were still blurry. He walked closer, but I stayed where I was, waiting for him to make the first move. I was too scared to even get up, but I had to. I waited for him to leave, but he never left. He stood stationed silently by my bench. I didn't have time for this; I had to go find a job. It was now or never, I told myself. The moment my feet hit the ground, the ranger halted me.

"Yes?" I groaned. But I knew better; that was no way to speak to someone, especially if I wanted to find my way out of this.

"Ma'am? Hai dei genitori?"

"I speak Italian, but I can understand English better. Do you mind speaking English?"

He nodded. "Where are your parents?" he asked in accented English.

"They died a couple of years ago," I lied firmly. "I'm here by myself."

"How old are you?"

"Look, I actually have someplace to be right now…" I started. That wasn't exactly a lie.

"I just have to ask you some questions. It's protocol, you understand?"

"Yes, I understand." I looked around anxiously.

"Tell me your age."

"I just turned nineteen," I mumbled. Another lie.

"What's that?"

"I'm nineteen, sir."

"Okay. And you have a home?"

"Yes. Yes, I do." I stumbled over the words.

He sighed. "I'll let you off the hook this time, because you seem like a nice girl, but these gardens have rules. It closes at six p.m. every day, and you were here after hours. We have security, but personally, I find it's a lot of ground to cover! So, please leave on time. We don't want to see you here again tonight or any other night."

I nodded and rolled my luggage as far as I could from the man.

I sprinted all the way to the center of Naples. It was everything I had imagined it to be—maybe even more. It reminded me so much of the beauty of home, except all the bad things we had in Calabria didn't exist in Naples. The water stretched for miles, glimmering, its depths such a deep blue, yet the surface was so soft. The orange, pink, white, and blue houses served as a mesmerizing backdrop, stacked upon cliffs or anywhere they could fit.

I suddenly realized how much I was getting distracted. I couldn't stop fantasizing about Naples, but I had to keep going, find a job, make some money.

Up ahead stood a farmers' market, brimming with all kinds of fruits and vegetables. The stalls were all painted a mint green, set out neatly in rows. It was set in a pleasant alley, warm and friendly. I had to eat something. The mint sandwiches and lemon rolls looked so good. Oh, how tempting the cubed watermelon was, and how sweet it would taste!

I then realized how much I had taken for granted, how much I should have cherished. I suddenly knew how Sierra felt as well, with her struggle to survive each day. I should have appreciated those simple days, where delicious food was always in reach, and I didn't have a thing to worry about. But all of that was gone so soon. The world had changed so quickly.

I should have known to appreciate those days of comfort. If only I'd known.

SIERRA

I didn't know what to do. The old woman was dead, and Romily had killed her. My shoes were soaked in blood. My heart was drenched with fear and rage and confusion. Then all of that vanished, and I was left with emptiness.

My first instinct was to run, to tear out of the house as fast as I could. My next instinct was to scream at the top of my lungs, hoping someone would come save me. It was one or the other: save myself, or have someone else save me. Naturally, I went with the more reasonable option, which was to run.

My mother had taught me at a young age to fend for myself. I guessed she was preparing me for her death. She had taught me to fight for myself, not to rely on anyone else to come save me. So, I listened to her faraway words, and I ran until I reached Jia, who was knotting blades of grass into strange patterns as she sat on the snowy pebbles. I beckoned for her to follow me, as I was too breathless to speak. Jia jumped up immediately; she didn't even need an explanation. When she knew something was wrong, she didn't waste time with questions. She was the kind of friend whom you could trust to keep a secret safe.

Eventually, we stopped running—and it turned out that we had just made a big circle. We were right back at Romily's house, back in the deep end.

"I think I have a right to know what's going on," Jia finally said as we stood in front of Romily's house.

"We'll talk later, alright?" I said to Jia.

"Look, you know I'm not the type to interrogate. But I volunteered to leave my family behind to go on this trip, with little pay. I'm supposed to help you, so just tell me what's going on."

She had a point, so I used what little breath I had left to explain my hypothesis. "Romily injured that little girl we found near the forest, and she killed an old woman. When I entered the cottage, I saw her body, and I saw Ackerley sopping up the blood," I explained hurriedly. But judging by Jia's look, I should probably have taken my time.

"But—"

"No, there's no time!" I shook my head.

"Then what do we do?" The last word of her sentence drifted in the air, as if she were too drained for anything further.

"We have to talk to Romily!" I insisted.

"I think you've done enough, Sierra."

"What do you mean?"

"I'm eighteen years old. I'm the adult here. Fleur explicitly told me that I would be the one in charge. And as the *adult*, I think it's best if we don't go into Romily's cottage."

"So, you're saying we do nothing about the fact that she just killed someone?"

"I guess we could call the police?"

"You *guess*? We have a murder on our hands here, and you don't know if we should call the police?!"

"Well, how do we know for sure that Romily was the one who

killed the women and injured that little girl? What I mean is, we don't have any proof, Sierra."

"Fine. You're right."

Jia's face grew more serious. "Here's what we do: we find proof, we call the police with the proof, and after the murderer is put behind bars, we find Chantelle. Let's go."

"Wait! Shouldn't we call the police first? We don't need to find them proof; they'll do that themselves. And while they're searching for the murderer, we can continue with our search for Chantelle. Okay?"

"Alright." Jia sighed.

"Why do you sound so sad?"

"It's just that I wanted to be the hero for something. I know it sounds silly."

"Don't worry, we'll have plenty of time for that later. Jia, we really have to go now."

Jia just nodded.

With the phone that Fleur had given me, I dialed 112, the European emergency number. Naturally, the dispatcher answered in hurried French. I hesitated, unsure of what to say, because I couldn't understand. Finally, I spoke.

"There's been a murder."

ANGELEE

I stuffed three coconuts into my suitcase when no one was looking. Although I had the money to pay for them, I knew I had to use it only when needed. I knew not to run, so I tried to act as normal as possible—at least, until someone shouted at the top of their lungs.

"Thief!"

And that's when I took off as fast as I could, my rolling suitcase trailing behind me, slowing me down. The reason I had chosen coconuts from the stall was because not only were they rich in fiber, but they could be used as a source of water as well. The only con was that they were heavy.

I ran down the alley as fast as my legs could carry me. A man was right behind me, his large belly bouncing as he struggled to follow. Then I realized with horror that the alley was coming to a dead end. I obviously couldn't go back, or even turn right or left. The only other possible way to go was up. But even that seemed much too ambitious as a red brick wall towered before me. It must have been about eight feet high. The crevices in the wall weren't nearly wide enough for me to slip my fingers into. So, I just stood there and let the man get me.

"Hand the coconuts over," he demanded.

I was relieved that he at least spoke English, and yet my stomach was churning with fear and guilt. "I'm sorry, I'm sorry," I stammered, "here are your coconuts." I slipped them out of my suitcase shamefully and handed them to the man.

"Okay, I'll let you off easy this time. But—"

"Oh, thank you, thank you, thank you!" I exclaimed with delight. I was happy then, but tomorrow I would feel even worse; it felt wrong to go unpunished.

"You live around here?"

I shrugged. "Yeah, I guess I call this place home now."

"Good. Come back to my stall every morning for a week. You must sell a hundred of these a day," he said.

"A *hundred*? That's a lot!"

"If you do what I ask, you'll earn eight euros a day. "

I nodded, thanked him, and walked away. *Well, I guess that's one way of getting a job,* I thought.

I was an organized person, to say the least. I felt incomplete without a list of tasks to finish. So, I had scribbled my "missions" on a scrap of paper after I arrived. Next on the list: I needed a new place to sleep. I guessed the houseboat would have to do for now.

The only negative was that the distance from the produce stalls to the docks was quite long, unless I found a ride.

"Hey!" a boy about my age called over to me from a sea-green convertible. He looked like a taxi driver.

"Yeah?" I hollered back.

"Need a ride?"

SIERRA

"I'll need some more information," said the dispatcher on the other end in admirable English.

"Okay, uh, the address is fifty-two Rue de la Hulotais. The potential murderer is a woman with red hair and freckles. Her name is Romily."

"Got it. We'll be there shortly. In the meantime, stay put, don't enter the crime scene, and keep a close eye on Romily."

"Well, what if she runs away?"

The dispatcher abruptly hung up. Apparently she didn't have time to answer questions, only to ask them.

Jia twiddled her thumbs nervously. "They're coming?"

"They'll be here soon. In the meantime, we might as well sit on the curb."

The snow was coming down even harder now. We shielded ourselves using Jia's sweatshirt. We sat on the curb for a while, doing nothing except staring at Romily's mother's cottage right across the street. The lights were only on in one room. Nothing stirred, and everything seemed so silent.

Then came the sirens, such a beautiful song. Policemen with polished badges and guns in hand soon surrounded the house. They stood stiffly, and I felt safe in their presence.

"Come out! Hands up!" they shouted. Their cries were barely audible over the heavy wind. Gradually, the policemen surrounded the house, their guns pointed. There must have been ten of them, all shouting. But when nobody exited the cottage, one of them attempted to open the front door. It didn't budge. All at once, the police officers started smashing the windows. It was a mess of broken glass, little shards flying everywhere, landing on the ground, slicing at the grass, and jabbing into the soil.

As the policemen stormed the house, it was as if they had been preparing for this day for their entire lives. They had. Romily and Ackerley were now surrounded. Their guns suddenly weren't for defense anymore; they were meant for shooting.

"It wasn't me, it wasn't me! I swear to God that it wasn't me!" Romily shouted defensively, breaking out into a bitter cry that cut the air, almost as piercing as the glass shards.

"One moment, I'm receiving a call," said one of the police officers as he answered the phone.

I listened attentively, my thoughts heavy. How terrible I would feel if it wasn't Romily who had committed the crime! And maybe when Ackerley was cleaning up the blood, he had only intended to help. What if I had wrongly accused Romily, after she had taken us in so kindly? How cruel was I?

"A policeman at headquarters is searching for your records. Strangely, there has been no documentation of anyone named Romily who lives in this town. We're going to have to run an image search to uncover your identity. The image search is highly accurate, but it may take a couple of days. In the meantime, you're going to stay at the station, with *him* as well." The policeman pointed to Ackerley.

I guessed this was heading in the right direction. They didn't know whether or not Romily had committed the crime, but if she did, they would first have to see what her real identity was. If she didn't commit the crime, then that would be a whole different story.

But it had to be Romily. It had to be Romily who killed that woman. And it had to be Ackerley. It had to be Ackerley who was her accomplice.

ANGELEE

"**I** never got a chance to ask your name."

"Oh, right," the young man said as he blasted the radio in his convertible. "I'm Ole."

"That doesn't sound Italian."

"Well, not everybody who lives in Italy is Italian."

"Oh. I've lived here my whole life, so I guess I just assumed that everybody lived in one place for their entire lives."

"Nope, I was actually born and raised in Norway. I moved here a year ago."

"Just because?" I questioned.

"No, no, I moved here because my sister is ill, and she needs help paying her medical bills. Naples had the highest-paying jobs, so I left home to earn some money."

"Oh, well, I'm sorry. I would love to help."

"You don't look like you're doing too well yourself," he observed as we pulled up at our destination. "Take care of yourself before you take care of others. And if you need anything, don't be afraid to come and find me."

I nodded and smiled as I got out, then waited until he drove away before I started to cry. I didn't know why. I was crying for Ole, for myself, for Sierra—for the whole world.

I raced down the dock to the safety of my houseboat. Guilt washed over me, and my mind hurt from thinking about all my troubles. Finally, it just got too tiring, so I allowed sleep to take all my thoughts away.

When I woke up, I felt my stomach aching bitterly from hunger. If only Ole were here to drive me to the center of town. I had to be there to work; I needed the money to purchase food. My throat was too parched to cry, my legs were too sore to run, and my heart was too torn to beat. I was helpless once again. The things I did for freedom…

I stepped out of the houseboat and walked down the dock. I was startled by the loud sound of a motor. I could make out a vehicle in the distance, driving right toward me. It was like I had wished on a star. Ole was really here! His car wasn't much, a mint-green piece of junk, but it could fly as fast as light, and it would get me to the central square. I didn't have to walk any further, or shout for someone to give me a ride; we would be there soon.

Everything would be good soon.

SIERRA

Jia and I had slept on the damp grass last night, the moisture from the snow soaking through our clothes. We couldn't sleep inside Romily's cottage, as no one was allowed to enter the crime scene. The sun was thankfully up after days of snow and gray clouds, casting a yellow glow over everything in the distance. I kept forgetting it was still late summer, because of the unusual weather. There we sat on Jia's oversized sweatshirt in the middle of a field by the cottage. How calm it seemed then, and how I wish now that I could go back to that moment. But the yellow caution tape around the perimeter of the house made everything feel a little scarier.

Jia lay next to me, her hands folded behind her head. She stared at the trees, her eyes following as they swayed in the wind. I bit into a peach I had picked from a nearby tree, its juice dripping down my hands and spilling across my lap. I didn't care anymore. I liked to think that I was away from the order and discipline that had once kept me sane. I let the juice fall, staining my white shirt. As I wiped my hands on the back of my pants, my cell phone rang. It was the police department. I picked it up reluctantly. Though I had been the one to report her to the police, Romily had taken us in kindly, and I didn't want her to go to prison.

"Hi, Sierra. We've done an image search for Romily, and we weren't able to find anything that links her image to her name. But we found another name that matches up with the suspect.

The image search took a shorter time than expected. We would just like you to know that Romily isn't in prison."

"Oh, thank goodness!" I sighed with relief.

"But Chantelle is."

ANGELEE

"**T**hank you, thank you!" I cried to Ole. "I promise I'll pay you back!"

"I already told you, there's no need for that," he assured me with a grin. And with that, he drove off.

The man who had caught me stealing the coconuts earlier ran over to me, juggling a container of freshly delivered produce. "Come here," he called, pointing to a worn and weathered stall with chipped paint. "Sell this box, and then we can have an early dinner. Okay? You can get started working today to make some extra money."

"Don't worry, everything will be sold before dinner," I assured him.

"It better be," he grumbled in response.

I was sweating by 2:00 p.m. Naples and Calabria had the same climate, yet I was farther away from the Mediterranean Sea, so the breeze wasn't reaching me. I worked for hours, and after a while, my voice got scratchy from continuously pleading with strangers to buy the produce. Most people continued walking, completely unaware that I was begging for them to buy something. Others who were kinder headed straight to my booth.

By early afternoon, there was a line so long that it seemed to stretch all the way through the town square. The vendor, Enzo, congratulated me on my success and declared that I deserved an early dinner break. He dismissed the remaining customers who were patiently waiting in line and told them to come back in a bit.

The meal was heavenly. Just the sight of food made my eyes water. Although the only thing Enzo had to spare was a slice of bread, sliced cheddar, and a halved cherry tomato, it still felt good to be putting something in my stomach.

After dinner, the line became shorter, which I was rather happy about. Enzo was obviously not proud, but at the same time, I was attracting more customers than he had ever had. From the look in Enzo's eyes, I could tell he felt ashamed of only paying me eight euros, given how hard I was working. Three hundred and sixty minutes in this scorching weather deserved much more pay; I was working for less than two euros per hour.

But at the end of the day, Enzo didn't feel any pity for me. He was already being too kind anyway, hiring me when I had stolen from him. He sent me home with two fresh buns coated in sesame seeds and a pitcher of milk. It was more than enough. After thanking Enzo with a smile, I walked to the heart of town, only a few blocks away from the produce stalls.

Right on time, Ole was there in his mint-green convertible, waiting for me by the curb. He had a scornful look on his face, with a hint of melancholy. "Get in," he said with a bitter edge.

"What's wrong?"

"They told me she only has one week left."

"What?" I asked, confused.

"The doctors. They called me up and told me that my sister only has one week left to live."

I didn't know what to say to that. I could've said something—

maybe how sorry I was—but I kept my mouth shut.

"So, where do you want to be dropped off?" he questioned, changing the subject.

I shrugged. "The docks again."

He nodded, and I didn't notice his tears at first because of how fast the car was going.

"Well, I guess this is it, then," Ole sighed as we arrived at the docks, as requested.

"I'll see you tomorrow." I grinned, trying to cheer him up.

"I'm leaving tonight."

"What? Where are you going?"

"I told you, my sister is very sick." The news from the doctors was definitely affecting Ole.

"Okay" was all I could muster.

"I have to go back to Norway, to be there with her these last few days. I'm leaving by plane, so you can keep the car. I don't need it anymore."

I was shocked. "What?! But you could sell it and use the money to help your sister!"

"There's nothing else I can do," he sighed.

I had never seen someone look so weak before. My heart broke for him.

SIERRA

"**I** don't understand, Officer. Chantelle is in prison? I thought Romily was the one who committed the crime," I stammered.

"Give me a moment to explain. Romily's real name is Chantelle."

"What?!"

"We ran several advanced image searches. We found out that Romily has been faking her identity. Her name is actually Chantelle."

"Do you mind telling me her last name?" I asked.

"Chantelle Toussaint."

"Lovely." I frowned.

"Ackerley will be coming home though. He's just a kid, and we know he has good intentions."

"How long could Chantelle's sentence be?"

"Well, the maximum will be thirty years if she's found guilty, but I'm sure it won't be that long," he reassured me. "There are barely any crimes committed in Blesle, so her case will be tried immediately. If we're lucky enough to have a kind judge at court, she'll be going in for twenty years."

The last part wasn't reassuring, but it was motivation—enough motivation for me to thank the officer, pack up Jia's and my belongings, explain to Jia what had happened, and run off to the courthouse.

Blesle was a small town. Everybody knew almost everybody else. The houses were spread far apart, yet neighbors didn't mind taking long walks to lend a hand or spare some sugar or a carton of eggs. The courthouse was in the center of town, just like everything else. It was quite easy to navigate through the scattered buildings.

The courtroom was not very big, as expected. There was just enough room to fit two benches for the defendant and plaintiff, as well as a raised bench for the judge. Chantelle stood behind a bench, and several officials stood behind her.

The judge frowned when she saw Jia and I step into the room. "Who are you?" she asked us sternly.

"We're friends of Chantelle—um, Ms. Toussaint," Jia said when she saw I was too numb to even say anything.

"Look, girls, I've already had a busy day, and it's not even noon yet. It would be better if you left. You can visit with your 'friend' after our work here is done," she said to us. Then to the officials she said, "Please help them find their way out."

The men pushed us back outside and closed the doors in our faces without saying a word.

"Please, let us in!" We banged on the door, hoping they would finally give in. But from what I could tell, the judge just continued with Chantelle's hearing, ignoring our pleas. Jia and I eventually gave up, pacing back and forth outside of the courtroom.

"We could try to get in through a window," Jia pointed out, trying to be of some use.

"It's useless. They would just kick us out all over again. For now, let's just eavesdrop."

We went outside and found a window into the courtroom, covered by blinds, but we could still manage to make out what everyone in the room was saying. We could just make them out through a slit in the blinds.

The judge took an odd approach towards Chantelle. Instead of asking the usual questions, she took a different path. Maybe the judge was just sick of asking the same things repeatedly?

"I'm going to make this quick. I don't want to be here any more than you do. Just tell me why you did it, if you did it."

"It's more complicated than I can say in a sentence or two," Chantelle replied. "I have to start at the very beginning for you to actually understand."

"Well, that's what we're here for. Commence," the judge said glumly.

"Well, I've lived here in Blesle all of my life. I used to live with my sister, Fleur, who now governs Calabria, and my mother and father, who have since passed. Seven years ago, we were on holiday, just me, Mom, and Dad. At the time, Fleur was in Calabria. There was an enormous cliff adjacent to our hotel, and below that was a large river that went almost sixty feet deep in some parts. My mom and dad and I all held hands as we considered jumping off the cliff into the river. We were doing it to make some family memories and relinquish all our troubles, as my mother had been diagnosed with cancer a year prior. We already knew she was going to die, and so she jumped, even though the doctor would have forbidden it. Of course, my father and I had no other choice at that point than to follow her. We jumped in together, holding hands, but then he let go of my hand. I plummeted underwater, and when I made it back to shore, my parents had disappeared. They had gone under; the waves pulled them in. They were never returning to me.

"Soon after their passing, it occurred to me that I was now an orphan, and I would have to fend for myself. I found a deserted little cottage in the woods here, and I hid there for years. Fleur believed that not only our parents were dead, but me too. I never answered her calls. There was an assumption that an unidentified body discovered in the water a little later was me, so that was proof enough. I eventually changed my name and dyed my hair. I was still in mourning, and I wasn't thinking clearly.

"Ackerley found me in that state of depression, and he proved to be of great help to me around the cottage. I promised to pay him significant sums of money in order to keep the secret about my identity. His family is not wealthy, so he kept his promise, and I kept mine.

"Years passed, and then Sierra and Jia showed up at my home. I don't know how, but they somehow found me, even without knowing my true identity. They informed me that they were looking for Chantelle. Of course, after all this time, I didn't want anyone to know I was Chantelle. And so, I told them I was Romily. By then it was clear that Fleur was looking for me. She had sent Jia and Sierra here to find me! I considered just telling them that I was Chantelle, but I'd been in hiding for so long, and I had no idea what was best. My mind was racing, and I was not myself. Something must have come over me…"

She was crying now. "Did I kill someone? Did I kill a woman just to get attention? Was it so Fleur would come save me?"

The judge was unmoved. "Continue, if there's more."

"This is the truth, as best as I can remember." Chantelle's whole body began to shake furiously. I could see the pain in her face.

"Bring those girls back in," the judge commanded, "and immediately call a doctor for Ms. Toussaint."

We heard all of this dialogue through the window, and we immediately rushed back into the courtroom. "You have to calm down, Chantelle, please!" I pleaded.

"I can't. My throat feels like it's closing up. It's getting harder to breathe…" She sounded so distraught, and even though I barely knew her, in that moment, my empathy for her was infinite.

"Call someone! Get an ambulance!" I cried to the judge and officials.

"I'm okay, I'm okay…." Chantelle stopped shaking.

"No, you're not!"

"I don't know what's happened to me, or how I could have done this," Chantelle stammered. Then without warning, she broke free of the police officer's grip and sprinted out of the building as fast as she could. Jia held me back as I tried to catch her.

"Give her a moment," Jia said solemnly."

"Don't worry." The judge smiled mysteriously while looking at me. "The officer will apprehend her soon enough and put her in prison, until she's in a better mental state to resume this case. For today though, she is permitted to stay in her residence with proper surveillance."

Jia was still holding onto me. I wanted to tell her to let me go, to let me run after Chantelle, but her grip was too strong, and my fight was too weak.

ANGELEE

$\mathbf{B}$ack on the boat, I caught a fleeting glimpse of the marvelous blue sea as my eyes closed softly. I had earned my eight euros for the day, plus buns and milk. There was really nothing else to do, so I let sleep overcome me.

I must've woken up a couple hours later. It was completely dark, but the warm lights outside illuminated the clouds. They seemed to fall into the abyss, slow moving and fast fading.

I loved mornings most. I would be woken up in bed by a butler, and breakfast would be served on a silver tray, with a cup of rose tea placed on a lace doily. But Sierra had never enjoyed that type of privilege, and I guessed that's why she preferred the night. She had told me she felt more alive during the nighttime hours, when no one could tell her what to do.

I wish Ole were here, I thought sadly. He was probably on his way to Norway by now. He had been good company. But at least I had a souvenir, and his mint-green convertible was just what I needed to get back to Calabria. I missed home terribly. I just wanted to go back, run into my mother's arms, and jump on my father's back. It had been promising here at first. I had a friend and a job, and I was making a little money. But I had quickly come to realize that I should have stayed with my family. I should have loved them more. I had managed to ruin it for all of us, and I knew that was all my fault. I had to contact them. I used the phone Fleur had given me to call my mom.

"Mom?"

"Angelee?" I imagined her sitting on the couch in our living room, sniffling in her sweater. "Where are you? I miss you, I really do. I'm so sorry I made you feel like you needed to run away from us. If only I'd known…" She spoke quietly, and I had never heard her sound so afraid before.

"Mom, it's okay. I'm sorry too."

"No, it's not okay! If only we could turn back time, I would've loved you more, would've been there for you. I missed the most special parts of your childhood, didn't I? I didn't even get to see you grow up."

"I wish that I had gotten more praise from you," I admitted. "I really did try. I tried my best at school and at home. I just wish you could've shown more appreciation and love."

"I know, I know," she sobbed.

"Well, the past doesn't matter anymore; it's gone. But we still have the present, and the future."

She sniffled. "But I'll always feel bad about what a terrible mother I've been to you."

"It's okay, Mom." I took a deep breath. "I'm coming back home."

"Oh, thank goodness!" she sobbed. "I love you, Angelee, forever and always. Some people shape you, and some people break you. You've changed me, Angelee. I see the world differently now. I see the important things in life more clearly."

"Even when I'm away, Mom, you're still there to throw advice at me."

My mother laughed heartily, then sighed. "I'll have a plane sent for you, my dear. And that boat you took off in will be returned with your apologies, okay?"

The very next day, I returned to the outdoor market where Enzo worked.

"Enzo, I'm afraid I can't work for you anymore."

His face reddened. "What, you think you can take advantage of me? You steal my coconuts, then I offer you a paying job, and you decide not to work for me anymore?"

"I'm sorry, Enzo. I truly have somewhere else I need to be."

I then handed him eighty-four euros and took off for the airport in Ole's green convertible, even though the driving lessons I once took, felt so long ago. "Keep the change!" I shouted. He went back to work with a grin on his face.

SIERRA

"Fleur," I said impatiently, "pick up, pick up!"

"Sierra? Is everything okay? I told you to only call me if there's an emergency."

"Yes, I know. And there is!"

"There is what?" she asked, without any idea that something terrible had occurred. She was probably filing her nails or sipping on a glass of chilled cucumber water. She had absolutely no idea that her sister was going to be imprisoned.

"There is an *emergency*." I took a pause to clear my throat. "Chantelle is going to prison!"

"What?! You found her?!" she cried out.

"Yes! And she's going to prison!"

"I don't understand. How can that be possible? Growing up, she was our parents' favorite. She was the good kid, the one who never got in trouble. She was just about perfect in every way. But she's alive? You're sure it's her?"

"Yes, she's alive! But she's done something terrible… We believe she murdered an innocent woman."

"She *what*?!"

"I'm speaking as clearly as I can, Fleur. I think it would be best if you come here and evaluate the situation for yourself."

"Okay, okay… I'm getting on a plane as soon as possible and coming to Blesle!" she shouted into the phone. "Book a hotel room for me, will you, please? Or just find someplace comfortable for me to stay."

"Yes, ma'am," I said.

"This is terrible! Her future is in jeopardy! That poor girl, my sweet sister… Protect her until I get there. Please, take care of her!"

"Don't worry, I'll book a hotel room, and I'll have Chantelle notified that you're on the way."

"Thank you. I'm just … just happy that she's alive! And I'm happy I chose *you* to go to Blesle."

"You never really did tell me why you chose me to come find Chantelle," I admitted.

"Sierra, I realize this has been on your mind. You were chosen because of your bravery, strength, and perseverance. Have confidence in yourself. Know your worth. I should be in Blesle by tomorrow morning, if all goes well, or around lunchtime at the latest. I'll see you then."

"Bye." I hung up and slumped down on the grass next to Jia.

"So, what'd she say?" Jia wondered curiously.

"She's coming tomorrow, taking the earliest flight possible. We have to notify Chantelle that Fleur is coming, and find a place for her to stay. It's been over a decade since they've seen each other."

"I would hope that Chantelle would be gracious enough to invite Fleur to her cottage," Jia said.

"That would certainly save us a lot of time and effort."

When we arrived at the cottage, the windows were shut tightly and the curtains were drawn. I quickly thought of the stable located in the back. When Chantelle awoke in the morning, she would hopefully check on the horses and find us sleeping there. This seemed like a better plan than knocking on the door and begging Chantelle to let us in. As Jia had said, she needed her space, although she was still being watched closely by the authorities.

We tossed hay over the floor of an empty horse stall, along with piles of grass and dead leaves. It served as a bed, although it wasn't very comfortable. The horses didn't seem to mind our presence after we gave them each a sugar cube. Jia slept silently, curled up in the corner. The gentle noises of the horses lulled me, but I couldn't quite find sleep. Finally, everything was quiet for a while, and I drifted off.

It wasn't long before I woke up. I hated when I was the only one awake. I often felt restless at night. I wished I could move, get up and explore. I envied Jia's peaceful slumber. Finally, I couldn't take it anymore; even the horses had lain down for a snooze.

Slowly and quietly, I got up and shook the hay from my pants. I exited the stable and headed towards the front door of the cottage. When I found it locked, I entered through one of the broken glass windows. There were several policemen positioned around the perimeter of Chantelle's property, but they were asleep, giving me the opportunity to enter the cottage.

Chantelle was seated on the couch centered in her living room. She was motionless, staring at the television, but she looked a million miles away, her eyes wide but lifeless.

"Chantelle?" I whispered, but I almost hoped she didn't hear me. I was afraid to wake her from her daze.

"Sierra?" she whispered back, her eyes still fixed on the television. The glow of the screen illuminated her sad face, which was damp with tears. "I feel sick to my stomach with guilt."

"I can only imagine." I swallowed hard, my throat burning like it usually did before I cried. "When are you going in?"

"The authorities expect me tomorrow morning. If I don't show up, five years could be added to my punishment."

"This is terrible. How did it happen?"

She broke down crying. "It's my fault, and it was an impulsive act. I wanted Fleur to know I was alive. I wanted her to save me from this life."

"You had options. You could have told Jia and me."

"It's not as easy as that though. I've lived much of my life tucked away in the depths of this forest—no friends or family, no meaningful interactions. I forgot what it was like to be around people. I didn't know what was real and what wasn't that day." She bit her lip.

"Why didn't you just come out of hiding?"

"I should have. Perhaps the trauma of loss had affected me. Months turned into years, and I lost track of time. Eventually, I didn't have the courage to actually explain to Fleur that I was alive. It was too late. She had become a ruler, she had become powerful, and yet she was fighting for me. I realized somewhere along the way that I was her purpose; I was why she became dictator of Calabria, and why she created those systems. At that point, I couldn't ruin it for her."

"Chantelle, she found out anyway. She found out that you're still alive," I pointed out.

"It doesn't matter that a few people know. No one else will know that I'm still alive, except for the policemen, Fleur, Jia, and you."

ANGELEE

It felt good to be home, for the most part. When my parents picked me up from the airport, they both had tears in their eyes and ran straight to me. They were just happy I was home, and it seemed like they had learned a lesson.

The days went by quickly. Fleur had broadcast her departure on the speaker at the municipal building to notify everyone that she was leaving. Yet she never explained why she was traveling to France. I suspected it was to help Sierra and Jia find Chantelle. I hadn't spoken to Sierra in quite a while at that point.

I found myself in our vineyard. My parents were at work, which meant I had the whole house to myself. There was nothing much to do, and I couldn't help but think about Naples. What would I be doing if I were back there instead of here? Perhaps in the morning, I would be at work, then I would be sleeping on the houseboat. Here, it was the same as always: boring and tiring. At least in Naples, I'd had freedom. Here, I had nothing.

Mother and Father came home from work earlier that day. I guessed they just wanted to be with me, to make sure that I didn't run away again. Father went to bed earlier than usual. I think he was depressed that I had chosen Naples over them. However, Mother was constantly by my side when she wasn't busy with something else. She made sure I had everything I needed, and for a while it was comforting, but after that, it just got annoying.

And then Sierra gave me a call, about a week after I had come back from Naples. I still had no idea what was going on with her and Jia. When she explained, it felt as if a huge weight was lifted off my shoulders. Thankfully, Sierra was okay.

"Angelee," she said, "we haven't talked in a while. There's a lot to catch up on."

"Yeah, same here."

"I'll go first, if you don't mind." And then she blurted everything out, like she had intended to go first no matter what. "So, you know how Jia and I were staying in Romily's cottage, right?"

"I believe you mentioned it."

"Okay, good. This will sound crazy, but Romily injured a young girl—and then murdered an elderly woman. And then we found out that Romily is actually Chantelle! She's been alive for all these years, in hiding."

"Wait, slow down! Chantelle is still alive?"

"Yes, and now she's awaiting trial for second-degree murder. Fleur is here now as well. She's trying to persuade the police to let Chantelle out of prison, using her money and influence."

"Wow, Sierra. That's a lot."

"I know, and that's why it's very important that you tell no one that Chantelle is alive, not even your parents. We aren't sure what will happen next. I promised her I would tell no one. Alright, now it's your turn to fill me in."

"I came back home."

There was a pause. "But I thought—"

"I missed home. I missed my mother and father. I don't like change, and I'm not good at adapting to it either. It's hard to put yourself in a completely different life. I had to come home to my normal life," I said.

"I get it. But if you had stayed a little longer, it would have been a good opportunity for you to experience new things," Sierra responded.

"Then you don't really understand. No one knows me at all," I whispered in a small voice.

"There are nearly nine billion people in this world. I'm sure *someone* understands," she said, trying to be funny.

"Well, out of those nine billion people, it's clearly not you." I hoped those words hit her hard. Maybe if she felt the pain, I would feel less of it.

"I have to go." Sierra tried to speak with strength, but failed. She hung up before I even had the chance to apologize.

SIERRA

Fleur was finally in France. She had arrived yesterday and called a limo to pick her up from the airport nearest to Blesle, which was quite small. I had asked Chantelle if she would be willing to let Fleur stay in her cottage, and after a lot of hesitation, she agreed.

The two sisters hadn't even met up with each other yet, despite being in the same small town for the past day. Fleur was busy at the police station, and Chantelle was in prison. However, today I had scheduled for Fleur to come meet with Chantelle for about an hour after lunch. Since they hadn't seen each other for a decade, I was very worried about how strained their relationship would turn out to be.

"Fleur! I scheduled you to see Chantelle from one to two p.m."

"Oh," she mumbled. Then she said quietly, "That's great."

"You aren't excited?"

"I'm not sure I want to see her," Fleur admitted.

"I don't understand this at all, Fleur."

"Listen, Sierra, I just can't be seen with a criminal. What will people think of me when they see me with a suspected murderer? I'm supposed to be their leader, and now all they're going to see is—"

"Fleur! I made a promise to myself that I wasn't going to fight you. Now I can't help but point out your selfishness. Your sister needs you, and all you care about is your image!"

"There's nothing wrong with caring about yourself," she snarled defensively.

"But there is a *limit*. What about others? Do you think about others, or only your own well-being and how you're perceived?"

"Are you crazy? My whole life is based on serving my people!" Fleur declared. "Sierra…" She paused, carefully considering what to say. "I don't want to create more difficulties. I'm very thankful that you found my sister, and a place for me to stay. I'm just uncertain on how to handle this unexpected situation. If you don't mind, I'm going to take a rest at the cottage after I talk to the police. I'll be at the prison at one p.m. on the dot."

"Well then, I'll stay here with you. I have nothing else to do, so I might as well try to help."

"On any other occasion, I would love your company, Sierra. But this is a private matter between me and my sister. Your work here is done, and after today, you and Jia will be heading home."

I frowned. "But…"

"Your dad is waiting for you back home, and Angelee is eagerly awaiting your arrival as well. You wouldn't want to keep them waiting, would you?"

"You don't even know Chantelle!" I protested, trying to change the subject. Fleur laughed. I added, "Do you even know why she's been in hiding all these years?"

"I think you've forgotten something: I know my sister better than anyone. I grew up with her. You know what? I tried to be nice, but I can't anymore. You thought I was evil, and yet you haven't even seen my bad side."

ANGELEE

I sat on one of the reclining sun chairs facing the infinity pool and let the sun bathe my skin. That was when I received another call from Sierra. I didn't miss her as much as I'd thought I would. Were we even friends? We had only known each other for such a short period of time, yet she was supposed to be my soulmate? Maybe our relationship was simply made of lies governed by Calabrian rules. We barely knew anything about each other. Best friends were supposed to know each other's favorite color and songs, hobbies and passions. But I knew next to nothing about Sierra, and fights seemed like a normal occurrence between us now.

I picked up the phone. "Hello?"

"Hey, Angelee, it's Sierra. I'm coming home tomorrow. I should be home by nightfall."

"That's wonderful!" I said, trying to sound enthusiastic. "Did everything go well? And Chantelle—is she okay?"

"Fleur is still trying to have Chantelle released. She's using every tactic she can come up with, but nothing has worked so far," Sierra reported.

"That's unfortunate. But I'm happy you're coming back home!"

After a long pause, Sierra said, "I wish I could stay a little longer. I didn't realize how much I would miss France and the experience of finally leaving Calabria. I also wish I could see more of the country, not just the small town of Blesle. I wish I could keep exploring."

"I get it. I miss Naples every day. I miss the freedom and the exhilaration of being in a whole new place. There was something about traveling someplace new that made me feel so enlightened. I miss it … a lot."

There was silence on the other end.

"So, what are you going to do?" I asked. "Stay in Blesle, or come home?"

"Well, I guess I never really considered staying here. I didn't think of it as an option. I assume Fleur has already booked the flight, and there's no point in me being here anymore."

"That's true."

"I have to go now. I scheduled Fleur to meet Chantelle today for the first time in a decade. I want to be there for their reunion."

"Best of luck. I have to go now too, someone's at the door."

"Talk to you later?" Sierra asked.

"Of course," I said before I hung up the phone.

There was no one at the door. Still, I wanted Sierra to think I was just as busy as her.

SIERRA

I led Fleur to the dark prison cell on the very outskirts of Blesle. Although the village was a charming place, this prison seemed like something from a horror movie. Concrete walls topped with spiked fences ensured that nobody inside could find their way out. The prison was small, with high ceilings and red brick everywhere.

A bald man with huge muscles stood beside the iron doors that led inside. Fleur and I held hands as we followed the man down a dark and surprisingly long corridor. Finally, a right turn came up, and an array of prison cells came into view: ten cells on each side, with metal bars separating them. At the moment, there were only four prisoners, including Chantelle. Crime wasn't common in a small town like Blesle, where mostly everyone was rich. So, it was quite a surprise that there had been a murder, and practically everyone here had heard about it. But they didn't know Chantelle had done it; they still thought the murderer was someone named Romily.

Chantelle was seated on a cot. It was big, but it didn't look comfortable. She looked sullen, her face blank and emotionless. But in her eyes, I could see that she was feeling guilt above all else. I knew she regretted what she had done, killing an innocent person simply for attention.

Chantelle didn't look up as we approached. Fleur wasn't much help either, tapping her foot impatiently on the concrete floor, waiting for her sister to make the first move.

Almost ten minutes of complete and utter silence passed. Fleur's visit was almost over.

Finally, I took a risk and spoke up myself. "Fleur booked a flight just to come see you. They aren't cheap, you know."

Chantelle sighed. "I know, I know. But is this what it took for you to come for me? Why didn't you call or make an effort to find me sooner?" she asked Fleur.

"I called every day, but you never picked up," Fleur protested. "I just stopped calling eventually. I thought you'd died. Then when I heard rumors that you were still alive, I sent two people out to find you. I don't allow that, you know; I don't allow people to leave Calabria. But I did all of this just for you."

"I wasted ten years of my life for you!" Chantelle cried.

"What do you mean?"

"The whole reason you became a dictator was because of me and my death. You created an entire social system because of me and my fight for gender equality. If I had just revealed to the whole world that I was alive, there would have been no point in your dictatorship or the systems you've created. I did it for you, remained silent for you … because I love you."

Fleur had tears in her eyes. "I love you too, Chantelle. I don't want to be a dictator anymore though; I've served my time. Now I think the time is yours. This is what you've always dreamed of, since you were a child: to make a difference, to fight inequality. I think you would do a much better job than me." Fleur laughed, but then her face became much more solemn. "I'm serious, Chantelle. You know much more about the world than I do, and you relate to the Calabrians because you've been trapped, just as they have. I know you can do it."

"I would love to, Fleur." Chantelle smiled sweetly, and I watched as life seemed to flood back into her.

Fleur cleared her throat. "There are no ceremonies in Calabria to induct you as our official leader, and the citizens can't vote; they have no say. So, this is it. I just have to broadcast your leadership on national television and display it in the town square for everyone to see."

"That is an enormous step. What will happen to you?" Chantelle asked, concerned. "What position will you hold?"

"As I told you before, my time is done. I've made mistakes, but I powered through. I cried, I smiled. I've made memorable decisions in this dictatorship. Now I want you to do the same. Don't worry about me; that's my job."

"So, we're going home?" Chantelle's face was alight with hope.

"I'm going to find a way to clear your name. We'll fly to Calabria in the morning. The borders are closed. No one's allowed in or out except us."

"Thank you, Fleur. I will pay for my wrongdoing by working to create a more just society."

"So, that's it?" I cut in.

"Sierra, you did your job. It's time to go home now. Thank you for everything." Fleur hugged me, and I felt safe in her embrace.

Once we reached Chantelle's cottage, we kissed the grass, hoping to leave our mark there forever. "Goodbye, Blesle. We'll miss you," we said.

ANGELEE

I didn't know why I was sent back to the municipal building again. Perhaps the system had made a mistake. Maybe Sierra wasn't really my soulmate. I had received a letter from them, telling me to arrive at 3:00 p.m. sharp on Tuesday. Luckily, it was summer, and I was home with no other plans.

Well rested and fed, I began the three-mile walk to the municipal building. It was closer to Crotone, where the Devils lived, because they couldn't afford cars, so it would take me a while to get there.

I hadn't even reached the end of the driveway before my mother ran over to me in her leather flats. I'd had no idea she was even home; she wasn't there for breakfast. I imagined her getting ready in the master bathroom silently, slipping on her pearl necklaces in the silver light without a word.

"Darling, let me drive you."

"Mom, I'm fine. I'm fully capable of walking a couple miles. I just need some time for myself, some time to think."

Mother sighed and gave in. She gave me a kiss on each cheek before wishing me good luck and walking back into the house.

I got to the municipal building at exactly 3:00 p.m. I stood on the front lawn, resting against a tall cedar tree. Suddenly, a woman with her hair in a tall bun grabbed me and pulled me into a dark shed near the building.

"Don't be scared, don't be scared," the woman said quickly in a soft, soothing voice. But how could I not be frightened? I was tempted to scream, but she put her hand over my mouth. "Shhh! We can't have anyone eavesdropping!"

"Then don't pull someone into a dark shed without their consent or any warning!" I snapped.

"Please just hear me out. You promise not to speak while I'm speaking?"

"Just tell me what's going on! If you don't tell me your name immediately, I swear I'll scream at the top of my lungs!"

"There's no need for that. Let me explain. I'm a good friend of Fleur, she sent me to you. No one is actually waiting for you in the municipal building; it was just a false story to get you to me. Chantelle is still in jail, and we have to find some way to bail her out. That's where you come in. I heard you're an Angel, that you have tons of money sitting around. We have to use that money to convince the police to let Chantelle out of jail."

I was indignant. "No way am I going to use my parents' hard-earned money! They work day and night, and we are not responsible for someone else's crime. Go find another Angel to beg, because I am definitely not giving you our money to get a stranger out of jail!"

"Please, Angelee. We need you for this," she said urgently in a small whisper.

"Why can't Fleur just bail her out?"

"Fleur is nothing without power. Chantelle is set to be the new dictator, but she's still in Blesle, where Fleur has no power."

"What do you mean, Chantelle is set to be the new dictator?"

"You haven't heard? From Sierra or anyone?"

"No," I sighed, "I'm not sure she thinks of me as someone she can talk to."

"That's unfortunate. But we really do need your help, and so does Sierra. Be the bigger person."

"But I'm not. I'm *not* the bigger person. I couldn't be positive even if I tried. I'm helpless, and a terrible person. But I'm confident that there's no way I'm giving you my parents' money to get her out."

"Fine. Well, would you at least like to know how much money Fleur would need to get her out?"

"Go ahead. You're not changing my mind though."

"A little less than fifty thousand Euro."

I sighed. "Ok, I guess it's possible for me to give you thirty thousand euro, but the rest needs to be covered by Fleur and Chantelle."

She sighed with relief. "Thank you, that would be very much appreciated."

"One more thing. Why did you pull me into a shed to tell me this? You could've just spoken to me in the building."

"The building is equipped with far too many security cameras and microphones. I had to pull you in here because no one can know that Chantelle will soon be the dictator, until Fleur announces it."

"That makes sense," I admitted.

But I never caught her name.

SIERRA

Finally, we were out of Blesle. Fleur had received the money required, and Chantelle was released. And it was all because of Angelee. She really was an Angel.

Jia was taking a separate flight apart from me, Fleur, and Chantelle. She was traveling back to China, and we thought it would be the last time we ever saw each other. We had sat in the loft last night, staring out the window at the curb where we once sat.

"I'm going to miss you," Jia said somberly.

"I'll miss you too. But we'll see each other again soon." We both knew that was a lie, but what was the harm in believing it?

"It's been nice getting to know you, even though it's only been a short time," Jia said, and I nodded.

"Remember that icebreaker we did back at Fleur's mansion?"

"Of course I do." She laughed to herself. "You were intimidated by me, weren't you?"

"No, not exactly. I just wasn't used to socializing. I've spent most of my time in the woods and by myself."

She smiled. Maybe she felt sorry for me. But I didn't need her pity; I was perfectly strong.

"Good night," I said, the only two words I could say to end the conversation.

Jia cast her eyes downward and didn't say a word. I didn't blame her; it was an abrupt end to the conversation.

I didn't sleep well that night. My body as well as my mind were restless, and there was a point where I contemplated getting out of bed and taking a walk outside. I was going to miss Blesle, and I should've treasured these days more. I was the only Calabrian citizen to get this opportunity, yet I felt like I had taken it for granted.

I got out bed; I had technically been awake all night. Jia was still sleeping, and when I called her name, she sat up glumly and rubbed her eyes.

"It's time to go," I whispered, softly enough that she could still have time to adjust to the morning light. "Are you packed?"

"Yep, everything is stuffed in my suitcase. It was a struggle to even close it."

I stifled a laugh, then headed down the stairs into the kitchen for breakfast. It brought back flashbacks of our first morning in Blesle.

Chantelle and Fleur were talking worriedly at the breakfast bar as they ate French vanilla muffins. Fleur had at least temporarily helped Chantelle, but there were still more problems to come.

"Good morning!" they both chirped cheerfully, trying to cover up their urgency. I didn't bother to ask them what was wrong. I was too tired, and I just needed some food to boost my energy.

"Good morning," I half yawned. I grabbed a parfait bowl from the countertop, brimming with berries, yogurt, honey, and granola. Hopefully it would satisfy my hunger until we reached home.

There were two private jets waiting for us at the Clermont Ferrand Airport, nearest to Blesle. They stood tall on the runway, their wings stretching wide. The morning sun was still rising, and the sky was streaked with yellows and pinks. Jia and I held hands, standing on the runway, staring at the jets.

"Time to go!" Fleur shouted from inside the jet. "The captain is waiting for us."

"Bye, Jia," I said. "It was nice getting to know you. You helped a lot. I'll miss you."

"I'll miss you too," Jia started, but then she was cut off by Fleur.

"Hurry up!" shouted Fleur impatiently.

Jia walked over to her waiting jet, and I walked to mine. We waved our goodbyes, and that was it. Calabria was on the way to China, meaning that Jia could have just taken the same flight as us, but Fleur had chosen not to do that for some reason. She most likely wanted this flight to be private, giving us time to think and discuss the change of dictatorship that would soon occur. After all, Chantelle becoming dictator was a big deal and required a lot of thought.

"Wait! I just thought of something," I interrupted Chantelle. We were already up in the air. I directed my question to Fleur. "You never declared yourself dictator for life, did you?"

"No. In 2322, when I became dictator, I only officially declared myself to be in power for ten years. It's now been almost eleven years." Fleur nodded sadly, and I could see that she regretted all the bad things she had done as dictator.

The flight was quick. In this modern era, private jets were the fastest form of transportation. They were all electric, and you could travel one mile in less than thirty seconds.

We arrived at the Reggio di Calabria airport around noon. After disembarking, we walked toward two large open doors leading to a scenic garden. Four wooden benches surrounded a cascading fountain. Beyond the garden was home. Large green signs with white arrows pointed in the direction of each province. The only way to get to them was via a small tram that ran through Calabria, sleek and white. It was long and narrow, almost the exact width of the tracks. I had to take a separate tram from Fleur and Chantelle, because my destination as a Devil was Crotone. Chantelle wasn't actually an Angel or a Devil yet, but since she was the dictator's sister, I guessed that was enough.

I waved *ciao* to Fleur and Chantelle before they left. I would be receiving a letter later in the day, explaining when to meet them in the town square for the declaration of the change in dictatorship.

The tram was completely empty, other than the conductor. Even though all the seats in the front were open, I preferred to take one in the back for privacy, giving me some time to think. More privacy meant more thinking, and thinking was just what I needed. I had so many questions, and so few answers. I needed solutions.

I looked out the little black rectangular windows. A small stream ran through the densely wooded forest. It bubbled with crystal-clear water, reminding me of the stream in the woods that I used to go to with my mother. The sun would soak us as we both bathed in the stream. Then we would lie on our backs on the boulders and just stare at the sky. We talked on and on, and it felt so good to relax after a long day of hunting. If only this stream I was looking at were the one in the woods. If only my mother were here with me.

The stream soon came to an end, and so did my train of thought. I sat blankly, staring at the seat in front of me. It hurt to think; I didn't want to anymore.

The track ran all the way through Calabria, by the sea, by the pier, by the fields. It also happened to run right by my apartment building in Crotone. The tram suddenly came to a halt, and as the doors opened, in front of me stood my father. I expected him to be much happier to see me, but instead, his face seemed subdued. He opened his arms, and I ran out of the tram and leapt into them. It felt so good to be home, to be with my father. At least I had him. He was a reflection of my mother. When I looked at him, I saw my mother's caring eyes, and it brought back the comforting feeling of nostalgia.

"You okay?" he questioned in a sullen tone.

"Well, I'm standing in front of you now. There's not a scratch on me, except from the thorn bushes in the forest, but that's another story for another time."

"No, tell me, I would love to hear," he said, now in a pleasant voice.

So, I told him everything, from the first day I'd arrived at Fleur's mansion to the second I got home. I told him about Ackerley, and Jia, and the icebreaker game we'd played, and "Romily," and her story about not wanting to ruin Fleur's purpose. I spoke of the loft, the murder, and the police. I hoped he believed me, but that didn't really matter; it just felt good to spill out the story to someone I trusted. I also remembered what Chantelle had told me: not to tell to anyone that she was alive. But she would become dictator soon, and the whole world would know she was alive, so it didn't matter if my father knew.

We walked up the stairs to our apartment complex, and then my father said, "Now what?"

"Well, Fleur said she would send a letter to me explaining what time we had to be in the town square. So, until then, we just wait. I think the letter is coming tonight."

"Sierra, I'm proud of you. More than you'll ever know."

"I didn't do anything," I said demurely, my cheeks turning a rosy pink.

"But you do so much, every day. When your mother … died, I wasn't feeling like myself," he explained apologetically. "I was supposed to be an adult; I was supposed to take care of you. You were only eight, yet you brought home food every single day. I wouldn't have survived without you, my darling."

"But that's what people are supposed to do: they're supposed to help each other. I just did what I thought was right."

"And that's exactly why I'm proud of you. It takes bravery—"

"But I'm not brave. I'm scared. You're my father; I had to go out there. If I hadn't been going to the woods for someone I loved, I wouldn't have even bothered."

He gave me a warm smile. "Still, you were there for me, even when I couldn't be there for myself."

"I know. But I doubt myself sometimes. I feel like what I'm doing isn't enough, like I should accomplish more, like there's more waiting for me."

He chuckled. "If there's anyone in the world right now who that applies to, it's me."

"But you work so hard, every day. You're the reason I'm alive."

"No, you're why *I'm* alive. You not only kept yourself alive, but me as well," he said.

"Let's compromise. We were and are in this together."

"That works too." He laughed.

I'd missed his laugh. It felt so good to hear it again. I used to not think about the little things, like the sound of his laugh, and the way his eyes danced when he was proud of me. I used to disregard those simple things. But after my mother's death and my trip to France, it seemed all the more important to savor the little things in life.

ANGELEE

When I got back from the municipal building, my mother was still home. Perhaps it was because she couldn't wait for my arrival. However, it turned out that her job had given her the day off, which was rare. She anxiously asked me how it went, and I replied to her casually that everything had gone fine. I didn't say anything more.

Two letters came in the mail that evening. It was nine p.m., but it was still light out as I walked back from the mailbox, the last rays of sun saying their farewell. And then the stars came out, a million little glowing dots.

One letter was from Fleur, and the other was from Sierra. Both must have been personally delivered to our mailbox, because there was no way the mail system would have been able to deliver them in such a short time. I went back inside and sat down at the dining table to read the letters. I read Fleur's first. She was still the dictator, after all, and it seemed more urgent.

Dear Citizens of Calabria,

I would like to thank all of you, Angels and Devils, for your sacrifice, your patience, your contributions, and your cooperation. Most of all, I thank you for bearing with me during the span of almost eleven long years. Now I ask you to please join me and support me as I transfer my power to the new leader of

Calabria, my sister, Chantelle Toussaint, on September 24, 2332, from 6:00 to 7:00 p.m. I hope to see you all there.

I know it has been a hard journey for you all, and believe it or not, it has been for me as well. I began the soulmate system because of my sister's desire for equality. This system began after I thought my sister had died. In her memory, I wanted to create an ode to her, in which her hopes would live on forever. Eleven years ago, it seemed as though the only way to create equality within our region was to enforce inequality, but it never worked out the way I imagined. I trust that Chantelle will do a much better job than I have. Once again, I thank you for making her dreams come true, as they are mine too. And I can only hope that you find it within yourselves to trust again, to have faith in a foreign leader, to have faith in my sister. Her aspirations are good, and the way she wants to achieve those aspirations is even better.

Sincerely,

Fleur Toussaint

I happily noticed that when Fleur mentioned Chantelle taking power, she said "leader," not "dictator."

The next letter was from Sierra.

To my friend Angelee,

I'm back from Blesle! Did you miss me? I'm sorry for not understanding your situation, for not understanding why you came back to Calabria. You could've phrased those harsh words in a different way though. Let's stop with the silly fights; I hate them. I arrived at noon, and I was surprised you weren't there waiting for me. Maybe we could see each other soon. We could meet up before we go to the meeting in the town square. I assume you're busy, so I won't take up any more of your time.

See you soon,

Sierra

I felt terrible that Sierra thought of me in such a way, that she was hurt that I didn't show up at the airport for her, and that she was frustrated about all of our fights. I was sure she wouldn't have brought those topics up if they weren't upsetting her. I wished she knew that she was already my best friend. I wished she knew that I didn't hate her, and that what I actually hated was getting into fights and silly arguments and making mistakes that affected her. I wished she knew. If only she could read my mind.

I gave her a call. No answer. I called again. No answer. I let the phone go to voicemail, and everything I was thinking in my head, I said aloud for the message to capture. Even though the trip to Blesle was over, Fleur had been kind enough to let us keep the phones. Keeping the phones meant keeping the conversation between me and Sierra going, and that was enough to maintain our friendship.

SIERRA

Angelee and I held hands as we watched Chantelle walk onto the makeshift stage in the middle of the town square. It was a beautiful fall evening, yet it felt more like summer. The clouds were beautiful, large and puffy, full and white. We were in the middle of the crowd, and we were forced to the back at one point, but we pushed our way back up again. Hundreds of people were packed in around us, but all were silent, numb. I expected them to be chattering excitedly, wondering what would happen next. But I myself wasn't very excited at all. Nothing new would happen. Things would stay exactly the same, only with a new dictator, a new name.

It was 5:45 p.m., September 24. The ceremony would start in fifteen minutes. We had come early because we wanted to reserve a spot, but obviously some people had arrived before us. My father and Angelee's parents were all standing together behind Angelee and me. There were no chairs; it was just a jumble of standing people. Luckily, there were two large screens positioned on the right and left of the stage that projected what was happening. A leader from Greece was also in the audience, because it was required by law that an official had to supervise the proceedings.

After testing the microphone's volume, Fleur began to speak. "Hello, citizens of Calabria! Thank you so much for joining us today on this delightful occasion. First, let us welcome to the stage my beloved sister, Chantelle!" Fleur motioned for everyone to clap, but the audience was unenthusiastic. "Continuing on, I would next like to welcome Aeolus Agathangelou, the president of Greece! He will be supervising our ceremony today to make sure everything is done properly. A round of applause would be nice this time."

Still no one clapped. Aelous walked up to the stage, clearly embarrassed that no one was celebrating his arrival.

"The next step is all about Chantelle. What makes her a good leader? How will she lead this region with strength and fairness? Let's hear from her."

Chantelle smiled nervously. It was the first time I had seen her pearly white teeth so clearly, even in the dark of evening. "Hello, Calabria. I'll admit, I'm scared, just as much as you. I've never been a leader; I've been in hiding for much of my life. I've been hiding in the depths of a forest. I've been trapped, like you. I was alone, and I'm sure all of you have felt that too. Devils, I'm sure you can relate. I was hungry, but I couldn't leave to get food. I had to grow a garden in my backyard, but it still wasn't enough to keep me thriving. Angels, you can relate to me too. I was pretty wealthy, with nothing to spend my money on except bills and taxes. All the money seemed to build up with no use for it. So, really, I am all of you. I will lead Calabria with the same mindset that many of you seem to possess. I will be strong like the Devils, and willing to share like the Angels. You can trust me, because I am one of you."

This time, the audience clapped. It wasn't loud applause, but it was better than silence.

"Wonderful, wonderful," Aeolus said. "Now, Chantelle, please just sign and date these documents. Your signature is only needed on the second page, and your date of birth on the third."

After all the documents had been signed, Fleur took them and sighed happily. But I did notice her lips turning down a bit, like she was sad that her career as a dictator was coming to an end. "And now, I give you Chantelle Toussaint, the new leader of Calabria!" Fleur shouted.

The moment should have felt good, but it just felt strange. I didn't know how to react—whether to clap or cry or smile.

"If you don't mind," Chantelle cut in before the audience could start heading out, "I would like to say something." Fleur motioned for her to continue. "My first act as your new leader is highly important. I'm choosing to enact some new laws because I've seen so many of you suffer, just as I have. I don't want there to be any more pain, especially when it's not necessary. Please film this, President Aeolus."

The president nodded, took his phone out of his back pocket, and started recording.

"I am proud of my sister, Fleur, for her role as dictator. But now I am the one in power, and I have the power to create change. Change is good, and change is needed. So, the Angels and Devils system will be no more. There will be no more soulmates or soulmate testing. Men will not be forced into labor. And finally, you can leave Calabria now, or you can choose to stay. I am not a dictator; I am simply a leader. I don't want to hold you back. I want you to have a voice. But don't leave me here all alone. If you all flee Calabria, then the empire that Fleur built over all these years will crumble. Please stay and help me build a new Calabria! Help me create a modernized system that values equality, without relying on inequality. But no matter what you choose, Calabria is now free. *La Calabria è libera!*"

And finally, the crowd went wild.